Special Thanks:

Victoria Nohelty

Maria Vargas

Roscoe Fay

Michael Fister

James and Susan Nohelty

Thomas J. Fortunato

Shelley and Grady Smith

Dorphise Jean

Victoria Kent

Louise Eklund

Elizabeth, Marc, and Nicolas Romano

Angie Simpson

Todd Good

Lynnette Prock

ALSO BY RUSSELL NOHELTY

THE SHITIVERSE

The Gods' Sin

The Immortal's Doom

The Pixie's Promise

The Devil's Circle

OTHER WORK

My Father Didn't Kill Himself

Sorry for Existing

The Little Bird and the Little Worm

Gumshoes: The Case of Madison's Father

The Invasion Saga

The Marked Ones

The Vessel

Worst Thing in the Universe

The Void Calls Us Home

GRAPHIC NOVELS AND COMIC BOOKS

Ichabod Jones: Monster Hunter

Katrina Hates the Dead

Gherkin Boy

Pixie Dust

MY FATHER DIDN'T KILL HIMSELF

By:
Russell Nohelty

Edited by:
Melissa Van Natta

Additional Editing by:
Gretchen Sparkman

Proofread by:
Katrina Roets

Cover by:
Charlotte Stevens

Dedicated to Sammy, he molded me into somebody that doesn't suck at writing as much as I once did.

WELCOME TO MY DIARY

Posted by Delilah Clark × August 25 at 6:30 pm.

I have Mr. Willis for fifth period English.

Ole Willy forces his students to record their thoughts, hopes, and dreams in a stupid diary for the whole school year. Worse, it counts for over 50 percent of our grade!

Everybody hates it, but it's sort of like a write (ha! get it?) of passage since he's been there for seventy thousand years. Even my mom and dad had to do it and they graduated during the Taft administration.

Well, he's in for a news flash: I don't hate this assignment one iota. In fact, I LOVE it!

I squealed a bit when the school mailed my schedule and I found Mr. Willis's name. I figured he would've retired by now or maybe even died. Worse than that, I could have been assigned to Mrs. Gropple's class, enduring her tedium is a fate worse than death.

I've been gleefully anticipating his class all summer, plotting how I will make it more exciting for me, him, and our entire class. While Alex, my best friend, was passed out at the foot of my bed during an all-night brainstorming session, I finalized my plot. She was, in fact, a great snoring springboard to bounce ideas off.

Here's what I came up with: I'm going to drag Ole Willy into the nineteenth century kicking and screaming. I know it's the twenty-first century, but I'll take bringing him into the 1800s. I seriously don't even think he knows about the cotton gin. From his lopsided pants to his ill-fitting shirts, I suspect his wife still knits all his clothes by hand.

But not anymore! Willy's gettin' with the times 'cuz I'm moving my diary online, people.

That's right.

Every thought in my head is going to be out there for digital consumption. Every opinion, picture, bad poem, good recipe—everything is going to be immortalized forever on the Internet. Since my life is already an open book, I don't even care if six billion Chinese kids read every word I have to say. I am slightly worried about getting egged by some of my classmates when I unveil my true feelings about them, but that's the price you pay for being an innovator.

Mr. Willis only has one rule for this project: we've got to be honest about what it's like to be a kid growing up in contemporary America.

That shouldn't be too hard for me. I don't ever lie.

Alex says it's my most annoying quality. She, better than anyone, would know; we've known each other since kindergarten.

I HATE THIS

Posted by Alex Dewitt × August 27 at 9:18 pm.

All summer I crossed my fingers and prayed for anything but your English class. Every year you make your students write this stupid journal that counts for over 50% percent of their grade. Fifty percent! That's crazy sauce! If I do a bad job on it, I could end up with 50 percent—that's an F! It's unfair and I don't care who knows it.

So, of course, my schedule came and I have you for English. Delilah flipped her lid in excitement. She planned literally all summer for the possibility and convinced (see: forced) me to do this stupid online journal with her.

Think anybody else in class has to do a stupid online diary? No. Just me, because I picked Delilah as a best friend in kindergarten.

Which is why I'm on this stupid computer. She's a steamroller and I m the concrete. It's better to let it flatten you rather than fight against it; eventually, it will just flatten you anyway.

So here I am, Mr. Willis. You swore up and down that we just had to be honest in this thing.

Heck, it's the only rule you gave us.

You're lucky you're the dance committee advisor and I want to be head of it this year, or I'd let you have it.

I better get an A on this stupid thing.

DADDY'S GIRL

Posted by Delilah Clark × August 28 at 6:29 pm.

I'm probably too old for this, but I don't care. I'm a total daddy's girl. I love my father more than anything. Don't get me wrong, I'm a huge fan of my mom, my friends, school, and a butt-load of other things too, but my dad's got a special place in my heart. In fact, I spend most Friday nights with him. We play video games on his old school Nintendo system. Donkey Kong is a personal favorite of mine.

Yes, I know I'm a bit weird. I like being a nerd, thank you very much!

We also go fishing, play football, and listen to awesome music. I mean seriously awesome 70s rock and 80s rap music, before it went all gangster. They just don't make music like that anymore.

I hang out with dad almost as much as Alex. It pisses her off royally since she can't get into trouble without me.

PUZZLES

Posted by Delilah Clark × August 29 at 11:34 pm.

Did I mention I love my dad? Pretty sure I did. I love him, and he LOVES riddles. He might love them more than a good banana split, and his cherry classic car combined.

He tries to stump me, but he can't. What's crazy is the fact that I've heard them all before. He only knows a few and he always says them in the same order.

I know them by heart at this point. Well, in all fairness, I knew them by heart when I was eight, but he's never stopped bombarding me with them. Plus, he's never bothered to learn any new ones, so I've had LOTS of practice.

If you ever meet my dad, you can make him think you're a genius by following this guide. Here are the only riddles he knows:

> Q: A man was born in 1955. He's alive and well today at age 33. How is this possible?
>
> A: He was born in room 1955.
>
> Q: A word I know, six letters it contains, subtract just one, and twelve is what remains.
>
> A: Dozens.
>
> Q: It walks on four legs in the morning, two legs at noon, and three legs in the evening. What is it?
>
> A: Man. He crawls on all fours as a baby, walks on two legs as an adult, and uses two legs and a cane when old.
>
> Q: Two in a corner, one in a room, zero in a house, but one in a shelter. What am I?"
>
> A: The letter *r*.
>
> Q: One would cost a quarter. Twelve would cost fifty cents. One hundred twenty-two would cost seventy-five cents. When I left the store, I had spent seventy-five cents. What did I buy?

A: House numbers! Stupid, old house numbers.

Q: Two as a whole and four in a pair. And six in a trio, you see. And eight's a quartet, but what you must get is the name that fits just one of me?

A: Half.

If you ever meet my dad, without fail, he *will* ask you those stupid riddles. He'll ask my prom date, my fiancé, every one of my friends, and every human being on the planet until the day he dies.

DINNER

Posted by Delilah Clark × August 30 at 9:21 pm.

There's this place in the middle of town that Dad and I end up at about three times a week. It's small and cramped, but it's kind of kitschy and cool.

The servers wear roller skates. They slide and skid on the marble f oor. It's a very poor design.

The new servers always fall on their faces, hurling tons and tons of food all over themselves and everyone else. It's glorious. The food is kind of good as well. The place is perfect, well, almost perfect. I seriously dislike the teenage jag-weeds that overrun it after school. Otherwise, it's perfect.

Especially the banana split. Now you might've had a banana split before, but nothing like this. This one's gargantuan. I think ten people could eat it and some would still be left over.

My dad and I aren't normal. We'll eat the whole thing without so much as a second thought and then order dinner as a chaser. Well, I guess dinner would be the dessert, because we always order the split first. Honestly, sometimes we don't even eat the meal. The only person I've ever seen who loves sweets as much as us is this bearded guy named James Nohelty. He would always come in and say, "I want…PIE!" Just like that, with the break and everything. Too bad he moved to Ithaca to start an alpaca farm or something.

No matter how we're feeling, there's got to be french fries. There's something about the combination of salty and sweet that just hits the spot after a long week. My mom's stomach churns when she watches us dip our fries deep into the ice cream, which is fine by me. I don't like sharing anyway.

They hate us too. I mean like vitriolic hate. If we didn't spend enough to single-handedly keep the place in business, they'd ship us out for sure.

But we do, so they don't.

Instead, they let us do things like stacking championships. That's when we pick a random number. Something reasonable like 5 or 10. Nothing crazy like the square root of 17 million.

Then, we run through the restaurant picking things that can stack into a skyscraper. The first one that can build a structure, with that number of objects (that lasts without crashing for more than 30 seconds), wins.

They're completely unstable and never last more than a minute. But it's super fun.

Not so much for the staff who have to clean it up, but fun for us.

Those are the days that Dad leaves a 200% tip. Money makes everything easier. I could punch the President if I donated enough to his campaign.

GYMNASTICS

Posted by Alex Dewitt × September 2 at 11:13 pm.

There are many things in the world I love: eating, watching movies, talking crap about celebrity dresses, and going out with friends. Classic basic bitch things. That's what I am. A basic bitch. There was a time when basic bitches were the queen bees. Britney. Christina. Mariah. What happened to them? When did liking simple things become so horrible?

I love one basic bitch thing more than any other. Like really love. Like really, really, really love.

Gymnastics.

Every boring, suburban white bitch does gymnastics as a kid. Most people grow out of it, height-wise or boob-wise.

I never did.

I've been doing it since I was five. I still pretty much have the body of a five-year-old, so I'm very good at it. I come in early, leave late, and practice on the weekends. I even dream in floor routines.

I can fly through the air with the greatest of ease. I'm a legend on the uneven bars. Despite all that, our coach never puts me in for competitions. I haven't competed in three months. Instead, our roster is full of boring, lame routines that get boring, lame scores.

Yeah, I fell off the balance beam last time I competed, but I was trying to do a one-legged crane flip. I tripped on the landing, but it would've been awesome.

Did the stupid coach warn me not to do it? Yeah. Did she tell me I had to quit using the bad ass tricks I invented myself? Yeah. Did she say I wouldn't compete if I did it? Yeah.

But it was soooo cool.

I landed it so many times in practice. I was so confident. And we were behind in points. The coach's lame routine would've gotten us third place at best, and third place is the second loser.

But this is a new year. And next competition, I'm gonna blow their minds.

HARVARD

Posted by Delilah Clark × September 3 at 7:18 am.

I have a confession. It's something I've only told a few people in my life: Alex, Mom, Dad, and my guidance counselor, Mr. Aldo. Some nosy teachers and a very astute gardener figured it out too, but I've personally only told four people. Now, I'm telling the whole blog-o-sphere. Here it goes.

I want to go to Harvard. I want to go to Harvard more than I want to do anything, even breathe. Although, if I stopped breathing, I couldn't go to Harvard. Hmmm...so I guess I really do care about breathing, but only in so much as it helps me go to Harvard.

I've been planning for it since before preschool.

I've only gotten one B in my entire life, and that was in stupid, sixth grade Home Economics. I highly doubt Harvard will look too poorly on someone who burned cookies and couldn't sew buttons back onto a sweater. At least that's what I hope.

Some nights I lay awake tossing and turning just thinking about it.

It has motivated me to work harder and push myself to higher, loftier goals. I'm already taking six AP classes this year, a record for a sophomore. It helps that I placed out of freshman English and Algebra.

I know this is going to come with a lot of ridicule at school. After all, people already see me as a bit of a brownnoser, so this won't do anything to stem my classmates' negative opinions of me. It certainly won't stop the rumors that I'm an Adderall junkie or a speed freak.

For the record though, I've only tried Adderall twice and I didn't like it either time. While my mind didn't wander at all while I was on it—and I was able to focus more intently than ever—being "high" in any respect didn't feel fair. I'm a pretty honest person and it felt like I was cheating the system. And I like the system.

On top of that, during my second "trip", I watched the episode of "Saved by the Bell" where Jessie downs caffeine pills and goes crazy. I know this is going to sound nuts, but it really affected me. I don't know if it was the abnormal concentration I was able to give to it, or the fact that I didn't want to become like her, but I never took another pill again.

Besides, I didn't really need them. Even with AP classes, school isn't much of a challenge for me.

Let me walk you through a normal test day in one of my classes. Math, Science, English, History, it doesn't really matter. They all play out the same.

The classroom is chock full of thirty or so bleary-eyed, frustrated students hung over from a late night of binge drinking.

One kid has a nervous breakdown. Three more stare out the window hoping they can soak in the answers from the sun. They can't.

Every few seconds, the sound of pencils scratching on answer sheets or scribbling on test papers can be heard.

Number 2 pencils of course.

You bring a Number 3 pencil into a test day and you'll be shot out of a cannon into the sun. I always kind of felt bad for the guy who invented a Number 3 pencil. He was so close!

Meanwhile, the teacher paces around looking for cheaters. Of course, the moment she turns her back, students reach into their pockets for a cell phone. It's an ancient game of cat and mouse, older than time itself.

Every time, the teacher gets a little savvier, but so does the cheater.

I see them—slackers, huddled in corners trying to find the best way to abuse the system. I wonder if teachers do the same. The funny thing is, if students would just put half the effort into studying for their tests that they put into getting out of them, they could get an honest B or better. Half of these cheaters will grow up to be thieves, the other half titans of industry. They'll all be criminals.

I sit above the fray in the front of the class, my character unimpeachable. Every teacher loves me. Several personally asked me if they could write my recommendation letter for the Harvard Early Admissions Program—when they found out of course, because I didn't tell them. It was my guidance counselor Mr. Aldo who let it slip. Teachers are notoriously gossipy after all.

I politely declined all but those with the best pedigree. You see, Harvard RARELY accepts sophomores into their summer program. But if you get into their summer program, you're nearly a lock to get into Harvard as a senior. And I definitely plan on getting into Harvard as a senior. So, I've got to work even harder than the other fools.

More than halfway through class I put my pencil down and smile. "Done!"

Grumbles and sneers come from all corners of the room. Sometimes there's a chorus of boos. Other times a wad of paper flings past my face. I don't care though. I have goals, and they don't involve any of my peers.

And you have to have goals in this world.

MARCO POLO

Posted by Delilah Clark × September 4 at 6:47 pm.

Alex and I have a really weird thing we do. Well we have a lot of weird things, but only one super weird thing.

We know it's weird, but we don't care. All the coolest people from history are weird.

We play Marco Polo in school, between classes. Well, honestly, we play it all the time, but it's mostly utilized in school.

I'm sure you've heard of it. Most kids learn it in the community pool when they can barely swim. Seriously, my mother taught me how to doggie paddle, then how to play Marco Polo, then how to swim for real.

I've searched around the Internet several times trying to figure out why it's called Marco Polo and not Christopher Columbus or Magellan. I found three possible explanations:

1. Marco Polo is easy and fun to say. Seriously, try it now and tell me it's not more fun to say that Cortez. The only explorer's name more fun to say than Marco Polo is Vasco De Gama.
2. Legend has it that Marco Polo didn't know where he was going when he set out on his travels. The name of the game, therefore, is an homage to him, since "Marco" has no idea where he is going in the game either.
3. At seventeen, Marco Polo traveled to China to visit the Khan with his family. Marco, exhausted from travel, fell asleep on his horse. Sensing this, the horse fell back from the pack. When he awoke, Marco didn't know where he was, but he heard his father and uncle shouting "Marco" and he began shouting back "Polo."

Now the first two explanations are very logical. In fact, these explanations go in order from what makes the most sense to the least sense. The third explanation is clearly the most convoluted. It's impossible to believe in all honesty. I mean seriously, who would shout back their last name when somebody was shouting out their first name? Especially when lost.

If I were lost and I heard somebody shouting out "Delilah!" I would shout back "Get over here. Hurry up and bring some potato chips!"

And it's in the spirit of that third explanation that Alex and I developed our own game of Marco Polo. It's really not so much a game, per se, but more of a homing beacon. Whenever one of us can't find the other, it's tradition for us to shout "Marco" until we hear the other one scream out, "Polo."

I used it when Alex ducked into a store at the mall and I couldn't find her. She used it when I got on the wrong bus and nearly took the midnight express to Atlantic City with a bunch of senior citizens.

But usually we use it in school. Whether we're walking past each other's classes or trying to find each other in a crowded hallway, we use it multiple times daily.

So, if you've ever heard a high pitched "Marco", or a higher pitched "Polo", now you know why.

GYMNASTICS

Posted by Delilah Clark × September 10 at 9:35 pm.

OH MY GOD!

Alex was amaze-balls tonight. Seriously, I wish I was half as coordinated walking as she is flying through the air.

Alex is a gymnast. A rad, awesome, super fantabulous gymnast at that, for anybody paying attention. And tonight, she had a match. Or game. Or, you know I've been going to those things for years and I still don't know what they're called. A meet maybe, or is that swimming?

Anyway.

I was seated in the gymnasium, waiting for her to compete. Who am I kidding? I was jumping up and down, screaming bloody murder, slapping my homemade thunder sticks together and hollering like I was being murdered by Freddy Krueger.

All the other gymnasts, from all the other schools, had already competed in the event. Alex was the last to go. The little Asian girl from across town was the winner in the clubhouse with a 9.3. She was really good, but she was nothing compared to Alex. Alex is a master of that pummel horsey thing.

Vault. It's called a vault.

I wore my favorite shirt—a bright-pink one with "ALEX IS #1" embossed on the front. I was a one-woman cheering section, shouting out every cheesy cliché in the book from "Let's go!" to "Be Aggressive. B - E - AGGRESSIVE" … and so on. Even though there were only twenty people in the gymnasium, I screamed so loud it sounded and felt like an Olympics gold medal match.

An old man, clearly the oldest person on the face of the planet, turned and glared at me several times. A woman and her child begged me to be quiet. But they were out of luck. Alex hadn't competed in a long time, and I gave every ounce of energy to support her.

She'd mostly slunk down in her chair until this moment, hidden behind her equally mortified teammates. I could tell she was embarrassed, ashamed, and even a little angry at how much a fool I was making of myself. I didn't care.

Alex's body is really muscular, even though she doesn't stand higher than five feet tall. Maybe even shorter than that. I'm about 5'9" and she barely comes up to my clavicle. I have a big head, too, so that adds a lot to my height.

Alex is strong and compact, like a pit bull or a bulldog. Pound for pound she has the most muscle on the team. I'd put her up in an arm wrestling match against some of the football players, even. Maybe not the linebackers, but she'd certainly beat the punter half to death. That's why she's so awesome on the vault. She can push off with so much force that her tiny frame catapults hundreds of feet into the air.

It's weird though, when she's not in the gym you wouldn't know she's packing those guns. She kind of comes across as a dainty priss. Now, I love her, so I can say that; if anybody else said that, I'd sock them in the gut. But it's true.

The only things Alex and I have in common are our unnatural love of pink and our natural blond hair.

That's right, I'm a natural blond.

Alex is much lither than me. Is lithe the right word? I think part of being lithe is grace, and I definitely don't have that. I'm constantly tripping over my own feet. That's probably why I don't do gymnastics. I tried it once and almost got myself killed. Now, I stay away from sports entirely.

I'm tall and slender. I tower over Alex.

And unlike Alex, I've got no muscle mass. Seriously, even carrying my book bag is tough going, especially with all the AP classes I take. I like to think I'm kind of pretty. Well, today I think that. I'll probably hate my hair, or my eyes, or my feet again tomorrow. But right now, I feel okay with myself. Wow, this is super off-topic. Back to the match!

Alex's blond hair, usually down to her shoulders and curly, was pulled up in a tight bun as she stepped up to the vault line....

Oh crap, I forgot something else. Alex is the best gymnast in our school. And I say that objectively, not just because I love her.

It doesn't matter that she's seventh on the team right now, or that she's only in the lineup because of sucky Jenny Dwyer having an injury. I hope Jenny stays in the wheelchair forever.

But even with Jenny at full strength, Alex really is the best, both objectively and subjectively. Not her fault she won't play the politic game.

Anyway, back to the story. As Alex stepped up to the vault line, she looked over at me, let out a deep sigh, and rolled her eyes. If my eyesight wasn't so amaze-balls, I wouldn't have seen the sly grin that crept across her face.

No matter how much she says she hates it, I know my enthusiasm is appreciated. It's not like anybody else shows it for her.

Alex was in position at the end of the mat and she closed her eyes, something she always does before a vault. I could see her lips move. She was performing an eight count, just like a dancer. Some people say the vault isn't graceful, but they've never seen the way Alex does it. She does, however, take forever to get going.

"Come on, Alex," I shouted, "while we're young!"

I'm always busting her balls like that. Well, she doesn't have balls. I mean those leotards leave nothing to the imagination and she DEFINITELY doesn't have balls. I guess I bust her ovaries, or her labia. Her cervix? Yeah, that's what I'm doing. I'm always busting her cervix.

No, that doesn't work either. Sounds like I took her virginity.

After an eternity, Alex opened her eyes. She was ready. Her eyes locked forward in laser-like focus. She is always like that when it comes to competition. And boys. Mostly boys. But mostly gymnastics. Once her eyes opened, I knew it was on.

Alex sprinted down the length of the floor really, really fast. Then she sprang onto the board and into the air. She leaped onto the vault, pressed off, and rose into the air, flipping and turning at least three hundred twenty-four times before she landed perfectly on the mat, shining her perfectly white teeth at the judges and winking right at me.

The crowd went wild. And by *crowd*, I mean me. I went wild. I hopped over the old man and the woman with her kid, right onto the floor.

Alex met me at the end of the mat, grinning from ear to ear, and hugged me. "You had to wear this stupid shirt again, huh?"

Alex turned. She watched the three stone-faced judges hold up her scores: 9.2, 9.4, 9.8.

"Is that enough for first place?" she asked.

I nodded. Tears started streaming down her face. She leapt into my arms. She hadn't won a gold medal in a long time.

I wish her parents could've been there to see it. Unfortunately, they're vacationing in Bora Bora for the winter. The whole winter. The WHOLE winter. It doesn't matter, though. I work super hard to be enough family for her.

"Hey, morons!" Jenny Dwyer shouted from her wheelchair. "There are still ten events left."

I told you she's awful.

I'm not going to cheer for her when she gets back from medical leave. See how she likes it.

WINNING

Posted by Alex Dewitt × September 12 at 6:13 pm.

I told you. I told you I was gonna destroy that competition. Oh man that amped me up. Oh man. Oh man. Oh man. The rush is ridiculous!

Let me paint you a picture of how hard it is to do a double-front flip and land on your feet without hopping.

Imagine walking with a rabid mongoose on your head, holding hydrochloric acid in both hands, all while navigating a tight rope lit on fire, and not spilling a single drop.

OR imagine you had to run really fast without tripping, jump onto a trampoline, flip over and find a coffee table to use as a springboard, flip over twice more, find your center, not break your neck, and land on a little mat. Do that all without tripping like a fool and do it with a smile.

It's a little difficult. It's slightly easier for me 'cuz I'm small, but not by much. I do a whole lot more calculating—and there is way more chance I break my neck—than some pansy-ass football player.

That's right. Gymnasts are better than football players. There I said it. And I am the best one of all.

BIDDIES

Posted by Delilah Clark × September 12 at 8:14 pm.

I've got a couple minutes before Alex comes over and we head to this god-awful party she talked me into going to with her. Why do I let her talk me into these horrible things?

Oh well, in Alex time a couple minutes is a couple hours. She loves being fashionably late. While I wait, I figure I'll drop some knowledge on the four of you reading this.

After the gymnastics match, I was milling around outside the school waiting to congratulate Alex on her big win. Spectators funneled out first, since the gymnasts wait until their adoring fans disperse. They wouldn't want to get mobbed, after all, by autograph seekers and paparazzi.

That was a joke.

There were only about thirty people in the audience, and t took them a grand total of thirteen seconds to fan out into the parking lot. Most of them were the families of one gymnast or another. They stood in groups, identifiable by their matching clothing and hair styles.

I go to a lot of these things and spend hours of my life waiting for Alex after her matches, or practice, or generally for her to get her butt in gear. If I don't do it nobody will cheer her on.

Since waiting is mind numbingly boring, my mind often wanders to the gaggles of old biddies surrounding me. They've taught me so much—from how to bake cookies without burning the bottoms, to where to find the best deal on Christmas tinsel.

But the most important lesson they taught me wasn't something they said; it was in the way they behaved.

Like teenagers. Seriously. From them, I learned my most valuable lesson to date. People don't really change all that much as they age.

Adults tell us we change and grow after high school, but that's a convenient lie. These women are just like the jerks I see every day milling about in front of homeroom and snickering at the weird, smelly kids between classes.

I watched as a clique of blondes in black peacoats poked fun at a group of redheads in blue blazers. "Tacky JCPenney crap," one said.

"Clearly last season," another mumbled.

Meanwhile, the blue blazers pretended it didn't bother them, even though their heads slouched lower with each insult. I almost felt bad for them. After all, the big dream every teenager buys into is that life is going to get better once high school is over. Without that hope, life is barely worth living.

So, we close our eyes and dream of being rich, married to our supermodel soul mate. That's definitely what those women in the blue blazers thought.

Unfortunately, reality isn't like that. Reality is a cold mother trucker.

And what's worse, those blue blazers were doing it just as bad to the mother wearing polyester pants and a ripped ski jacket.

"What is this, the '70s?" one of them said. Another one snickered.

And another nodded vigorously. "I wouldn't be caught dead in that."

It's like that old theory about kicking the dog. The CEO yells at the VP, who in turn yells at the supervisor, who yells at the office drone, who yells at the mail room guy, who yells at the cafeteria worker. The cafeteria worker goes home and yells at her daughter, who yells at her younger brother. And with nobody beneath him, he would have no choice, but to turn around and kick the dog.

No matter how low people are on the totem pole, they can always kick somebody underneath them. Just like high school.

I suppose that dog would then chase the cat, who would eat a rat, whose siblings would swear vengeance. The kick-the-dog theory has always sort of sickened me, but that doesn't make the gears of the world turn any differently.

It's a tough pill to swallow.

JENNY'S PARTY

Posted by Delilah Clark × September 13 at 2:51 am.

Why on Earth would we go to Jenny Dwyer's party? Two reasons.

1. To rub Alex's gold medal in her disabled face.
2. Because there's not much to do in East Willow on a Saturday night. It's Jenny's or picking our toenails, and my toenails are pristine.

That didn't mean it wasn't going to suck. In fact, it practically guaranteed it.

And it did suck. It super sucked. Like if suck was bit by a radioactive spider.

You know a party's not going to end well when the knot of dread in the pit of your stomach swells to the size of a watermelon. Psychologists might say I'm bound to have a terrible time because of my terrible attitude, but I don't lend too much credence to what a bunch of Oedipus-obsessed quacks believe.

Most people don't like Jenny, but her parents are cool with her drinking. That, and that alone, makes her popular, if you consider being used for alcohol popular that is.

I do, but it is a very sad popularity. Very sad indeed.

I've got to say, though, this whole post makes it seem like I hate parties, which couldn't be further from the truth. But there are good parties and bad parties.

See, I like people well enough. Individual people. An individual person is awesome. And I enjoy going places where you can meet individual people and talk with them. Parties like that are awesome.

Jenny's parties aren't like that, though. At Jenny's parties, an individual person becomes a slew of people. And people suck. They become howling, inconsiderate jack-holes. Add alcohol and that magnifies sevenfold.

By the time Dad pulled the Chevy up in front of Jenny's two-floor colonial, I'd slumped over the dashboard with a dread-induced, watermelon baby kicking my insides to bits. I named this one Leeroy, after Leeroy Jenkins, the greatest WoW player in existence.

My last watermelon baby was named Lucy, for Lucy Liu. I think my next one will be Michonne, the baddest chick in comics. I really didn't want to go tc this stupid party, but I had no choice.

Dad pulled me close and squeezed me tighter than he had in a long time. "I love you, kiddo."

"I know, Dad. I love you too. But I can't breathe."

I thought I saw a tear fall down his cheek as he released me. It must've been a glint of moonlight though, since my dad hasn't cried in the whole sixteen years I've known him.

It didn't take long after we got inside for Alex to grab a red solo cup filled with jungle juice.

Oh my God, you probably don't know what jungle juice is, do you? You can read about it online, but that won't do it justice. At least not the way Jenny's family does it.

It's basically rat poison. You start off with fruit punch and pour in any cheap, nasty alcohol you can find. If you're cool, which Jenny's mom swears they are, then you use 50% punch and 50% alcohol. It's a recipe for disaster if you have more than one. I call it Rape Juice.

We hadn't been there five minutes before Alex's mouth turned red, which meant she, Alex, had had at least two cups of rape juice and was quickly working through her third.

I don't like to drink much, but if I nurse one cup all night nobody is the wiser. In fact, by about eleven o'clock I can switch out the booze with water and everybody will be too wasted to notice, especially Alex.

Oh, Alex. From prior experience I know two things:

1. Five minutes after coming into a party, she is going to be dancing on a table.

2. If I don't keep a careful eye out, she is going to go off with the first guy that looks at her.

Right then, as if on cue, some rap song with a terrible beat blasted over the speakers and Alex's face lit up. She let go of my hand, finished her drink, and hopped up onto the table.

Graceful as she is on the gym mat, get a couple drinks in her and she moves like a water buffalo. I thought she was going to kick this jack-hole in an orange hat right in the face. And if he hadn't been eying her so attentively, she probably would have succeeded.

Too bad she didn't, in retrospect.

As dangerous as it is to dance on a table completely obliterated, at least she had a mosh pit of eager admirers to catch her should she fall. I just had to make sure I was there to pull them off of her before they got too handsy. I don't know what it is about a drunk girl that makes guys think she's a living sex doll. Guys are disgusting.

As I watched, less transfixed and more just oddly curious at how utterly uncoordinated Alex became after a few cups of cheap vodka, I noticed a large, bushy Afro headed my way. I knew exactly who owned it, and if there was one person I didn't want to see at this party, even more than Jenny, it was him. I looked for somewhere to hide but found none. I would be forced to deal with him: Moses.

Who is Moses you ask? Not the guy from the Bible, though he can part a sea of people with his unpopularity. He's this really weird kid that shows up in the most inopportune places. He's got a face for radio and a voice for print, as my dad would say. Too tall to fit well into even Jenny's enormous house, and too awkward not to bump into everyone as he made a beeline for me.

"Delilah!" he shouted, waving his hands. "I can't believe you came. Your feud with Jenny is legendary."

He wasn't invited. Nobody would invite him anywhere. He just walks into places and acts like he belongs. It works, though. Jenny's friends are so bleary-eyed and wasted, they wouldn't know who Moses was if he told them in a PowerPoint presentation filled with pictures of his crusty, ole face.

"Go away, Moses," I replied, pushing him aside so I could keep an eye on Alex.

That's when things got bad. He distracted me for like two seconds. Two flippin' seconds was all it took though. I looked toward the table, but Alex wasn't there anymore. I birthed my baby, its twin, and miscarried two more.

I immediately went on RED ALERT. The worst thing that could happen at any party was to lose complete sight of Alex, even for a moment.

I pushed Moses aside and marched up to the group of jack-holes in the dining room. The jerk in the orange baseball hat was conspicuously absent. I swear to God every guy is five drinks and a nearly unconscious girl from being a rapist.

Moses followed silently as I ping-ponged from room to room looking for Alex. I kicked myself for not listening to my watermelon baby as I searched the kitchen, bathrooms, front yard, and backyard.

I finally stopped to take a breath when I heard something. The unmistakable moaning of a girl coming from the master bedroom.

I bolted up the stairs and crashed through the door. There they were. Alex and that orange-hatted pig on the bed. Coats strewn on the floor. She was barely conscious, wearing nothing but underwear. He refused to take off that hat even when he was half naked.

Her skirt was crumpled up on the floor, where it had been thrown haphazardly. Orange hat was preparing to grind on her. "Get off of her!" I screamed at him.

"Get out of here!" he screamed. "She wants it."

I jumped on his back. Moses tugged at his leg. But even with both of us on him, he easily pushed us aside.

People funneled into the room to check out the commotion. They laughed and cheered like right idiots. None of them helped. Nobody except for Moses.

I wrapped myself around orange hat's chest and pulled as hard as I could, but it barely phased him. He actually laughed. "Get off her!" I screamed.

But he just laughed again. "What? You jealous, baby? I've got plenty for you as well."

He turned around and kissed me full on the lips. That jack-hole actually kissed me! Well I had had it at that point. I wound up and smacked him across the face. Moses leapt across the bed and tackled him to the ground.

The group gasped in horror. Orange Hat and Moses rolled onto the floor. They were screaming, punching each other, and knocking everything over.

I kicked him once in the gut for good measure, then hopped over him to Alex.

"Mom?" she asked, completely out of it. I redressed her and slung her arm around my shoulder. I turned back to Moses, who screamed "Go!" before Orange Hat punched him in the face.

And we did. God help me. We got out of there as quickly as possible. I have no idea what happened to Moses, but I'm really grateful for his help.

WALKING HOME – PRIVATE

Posted by Delilah Clark × September 13 at 1:08 pm.

I had more things I wanted to say about the party, but they're super embarrassing and I don't want anybody to find them out, ever. Still, I want to be honest, so I set this to private.

I walked Alex out of the party as quickly as her drunken feet could carry her. A couple of people stopped to ask if we needed a ride, but I declined. Alex almost getting raped made me kind of leery about accepting help from strangers, even though, rationally, I know it wasn't their fault.

I know we could've called my dad, but that whole, "Don't drink and if you do, call me for a ride home" crap is the worst parental entrapment west of the Mississippi.

We actually did call once, back when I was drinking more, and Alex was drinking, well, about equal to what she did tonight. And true to his word he picked us up and didn't even yell—until the next morning.

Then he let out a tirade the likes of which you wouldn't believe. "You're shaming this house.", "How could you be so stupid?", "I woke up at two in the morning.", "I thought you were more responsible." and much more, all poured out of his mouth in the course of the hour-long blitzkrieg. Ironically, it really made me want a stiff drink.

I'd been struggling with Alex's drunkenness almost the entire walk. About three blocks from home, my arms finally gave out. It's only about a mile from Jenny's house to mine, as the crow flies, but I'm not winning any weight lifting or stamina competitions any time soon— and carrying 103 pounds of dead weight made my arms burn something fierce. I'll venture a bet that Alex isn't going to like me revealing her weight like that but screw it. I'm tired and cranky.

Anyway, about three blocks from my house Alex slipped out of my arms and fell onto the street. Luckily, she didn't seem that broken up about it, skinned knees and all. In fact, she thought it was hilarious, hooting and hollering in that stupid way only drunks can laugh.

After about thirty seconds of raucous guffawing on her part, and a couple bedroom lights flipping on, I had had enough. "Would you shut up?" I asked. "You're going to wake my neighbors."

She was in a drunken daze and stumbled to stand. "They can suck it. I have…I've got to pee."

Again, we were three blocks from my house. She could have crawled to a bathroom in three minutes, but she couldn't help it. She looked at me, eyes glazed over. I could see the gerbil running around in her brain trying to make the connection, but the wheels weren't spinning.

"I've got to pee."

Alex crawled haphazardly into the bushes. She pulled down her underwear and started peeing, like a dog, into Mrs. Turnbell's hydrangeas.

Is she an animal? She must be an animal. She reminded me of Maria Vargas's miniature schnauzer. He loves Mrs. Turnbell's flowers. Maria walks him three times a day, all over the neighborhood, and he always pees in those same flowers.

I dropped my head into my hands and turned away. I focused on one of the flickering, overhead street lamps. My dad had called the county about fixing it, but there was no budget to hire an electrician. He had tried to climb up the pole himself but fell at least twenty times before giving up.

I wondered how many epileptic vampires have had a stroke in the street while they stumbled home to their coffins before sunrise.

As I pondered this, a dark, sinewy figure emerged from the darkness. It was Jeremiah, my next-door neighbor. I'd recognize him even half a mile away. He's the only idiot prowling the streets past midnight.

The stench of his matted and unwashed hair wafted in front of him like a chemical weapon. If I believed in vampires, epileptic or not, I might be convinced that Jeremiah was one. After all, he is pasty-skinned, and he only comes out at night.

Don't worry though, this isn't one of those stories. I'm not falling in love with the thousand-year-old sparkly vampire with the bad attitude. I don't even see what a thousand-year-old sparkly vampire would have to talk about with a sixteen-year-old. I mean seriously, imagine trying to have a conversation with your grandfather. How much do you two have in common? About as much as a mongoose and a garden snake, right?

Jeremiah lit a cigarette as he approached. Though it did mask the scent of his musk, I hate the smell of cigarettes more than books about sparkly vampires. Seriously, who smokes anymore? I mean, who can even afford it? A pack of cigarettes by my house just hit $7.50. That means if you smoked a pack a day, you'd be spending $52.50 a week. That's $2730 a year. A year! You're just pissing money away at that point. Just give that money to me, I'll find a much cooler use for it, like hiring a Zorbing company to personally push you around for a week.

Jeremiah stood in front of me for a few seconds before opening his pie hole. "Smoke?"

"Never touch the stuff."

"Better for you that way. I'm thinking about quitting to buy a jet ski."

"You can't pull a jet ski to the lake with your car."

I turned and saw Alex writhing around like a turtle on its back, trying to pull up her underwear. If she were Paris Hilton, somebody would've gotten a great shot of her. Luckily, nobody cares about the people of East Willow.

I ran over and helped Alex to her feet. I pulled up her underpants. Man, I never thought I'd have to write that sentence.

I dragged Alex away as quickly as possible, which was actually quite slow. Jeremiah watched the whole thing, giggling to himself like a schoolgirl.

It took me 30 more minutes to drag her home, but she fell asleep the second she hit the couch.

It was exhausting.

Sometimes I hate her so much I love her again.

Unlike Jeremiah, who I just hate.

HANGOVER

Posted by Alex Dewitt × September 13 at 5:23 pm.

Honesty, huh? That's what you're after. That's what's going to get me my A?

You're completely sure honesty is the thing you want, huh? Because I'm going to be honest. If I get in trouble, I'm blaming you.

I got hammered last night. I'm not usually that big a drinker. I mean I like a few drinks here and there, but I always maintain.

Well, I usually maintain. Last night I was celebrating my gold medal, my victory, so I let loose.

I don't know why drinking is such a big deal anyway. I mean honestly, in Europe toddlers suck on wine bottles like they're juice boxes. But somehow in America, we're too prudish to hook that up, so now I'm some delinquent for having a couple cocktails?

I'm not a delinquent. I get decent grades. Not great, but good enough. Good enough for my parents. Good enough for me. So what if I stay out late and drink a little. What does it matter that I (sometimes) dress provocatively and dance on tables?

My best friend is wound so tight sometimes her tension rubs off on me and I need a release. It's not like I'm out gang-banging soccer players during a bender. I just like to dance. I like to have fun. I like to let loose.

Lord knows Monday to Friday there's not much time for that. Mr. Willis, you give us so much homework, that sometimes I'm up until 11:30 *just* on your assignments. That's stressful. Gymnastics helps, but I can't use a vaulting table in the comfort of our house. I can have a glass of scotch though.

Considering both of my parents are out the country half the year, sneaking the occasional glass of booze is minor on the scale of potential craziness I could get up to.

I paid for it today though. I couldn't get out of bed until an hour ago. I couldn't roll over until three hours ago. I was in so much pain. You'd think that would be enough for me to learn my lesson.

It's not.

I'll do it again.

Why? Because I'm a glutton for punishment and a slave to the music.

DAD'S CHERRY RIDE

Posted by Delilah Clark × September 15 at 3:13 pm.

I have to tell you about my dad's car, his '57 Chevy. The love of his life. Seriously, he probably loves that car more than anything in the world. Well, with the possible exception of my mother and me, but it's a really close race.

Now let me preface this by again by saying how much I love my dad. Aside from Alex he's the person I most relate to in the world. We hang out all the time. Like *all* the time. I think I made this clear already, but I'll state it again for the record.

He's gentle and considerate. He pays his taxes, gives to charity, and is genuinely fun to be around. We can talk for hours about nothing and still have a great time. But just like some things cheese me off royally about Alex, that car pisses me off about him more than anything.

That's not to say it's ugly. It's a cherry ride. It's just everything about it pisses me off. Especially the horn.

There's nothing about that car he gets a kick out of more than the horn. That friggin' horn. It grates on me every time I hear it. It's the first thing anybody notices when he pulls up because he honks it every chance he gets. He got one of those novelty horns that plays "The Mexican Hat Dance".

Are we Mexican? Nope. I couldn't be whiter. My ancestors were Finnish, Swiss, German, and some sort of Czech hybrid. I'm not 100 percent sure there isn't anything else in there, and I guess some part of it could be Mexican, but nothing statistically significant.

Has he ever been to Mexico? Nope. He hasn't left town more than three times since I've been born. So why does he have "The Mexican Hat Dance" as his car horn? Your guess is as good as mine.

It's funny because there's an actual mariachi band at the Mexican restaurant in town that plays every Saturday. We went there once, and I literally paid them to play "The Mexican Hat Dance" for him. When they finished, he shrugged and said he liked the horn better. I was flabbergasted; all I could do was eat my flautas in silence.

There's a reason the car is so cherry. It had to be.

I mean he spent three years systematically searching for it. Seriously, three flippin' years!

The tail fins had to be the right length. The wheels had to be whitewashed. And the color. He insisted on powder blue. I can't tell you how many great cars he turned down just because of the color. It's the color that keeps him outside waxing it every Saturday. It's the color he talks about ad nauseum. It's the color that makes him swoon.

Not to mention that just buying the car was a huge production in and of itself. That car caused more fighting between my mom and dad than everything else in our lives combined. Finances, coming home late, what's for dinner, "your butt looks fat in that dress"—all that crap pales in comparison to the bare-knuckle, knock-down, drag-out fights that that car initiated.

My dad has never turned away from a fight. He's as stubborn as a mule when he wants something. But I've never seen him act as pig-headed as he did with Yvette. Yes, the car's name is Yvette. I think it's ridiculous to name an American-made, muscle car Yvette, but that's what guys do. I've always thought of it as a George. It looks like a George.

"George was impractical," my mom said. *"He was expensive,"* she said. *"We needed the money for other things,"* she said. *"He guzzled gas,"* she said. *"He was uncomfortable,"* she said. *"I can't drive a stick,"* she said.

But my dad didn't care. *"It's my money,"* he said. *"I work hard,"* he said. *"I deserve nice things,"* he said. *"I've wanted this my whole life,"* he said.

Eventually, he bought it anyway, without permission. That went over well. One day he parked it in the driveway, grinning from ear to ear. I swore my mom was going to grab the knife she'd been dicing tomatoes with and stab him in the throat, on the spot.

That wasn't a fun night to be a Clark.

I locked myself in my room when the fighting became too much for me. At two in the morning, they were still going strong. I snuck out my window, crept into Alex's house, and slept on her floor.

It wasn't the first time we'd done that. It won't be the last. It seems to happen most frequently when Alex's parents are out of town. She won't admit it, but she's scared of the dark. And her big house creaks all night, making her swear it's haunted. If my being there helps stem the loneliness of her world, then I'll be there any time she needs.

Maybe that car helps stem my dad's loneliness.

HOMESTEAD

Posted by Delilah Clark × September 20 at 1:53 am.

My house is nothing like Jenny's, but it's no crack house either. I talk down about it sometimes, but who doesn't have negative thoughts about their house every now and then?

I'll bet even the President thinks his house is a piece of junk sometimes. He'd probably say, "Why do I have to walk all the way down to the kitchen when I want a banana scone at three in the morning?" and "Isn't there any heat in this place?" after stepping on the cold tile in the bathroom.

If my house isn't even good enough for Jenny Dwyer, it's definitely no White House. It isn't without its endearing qualities, though. For one thing, I think this is the only piss-yellow house with menstrual-red shutters in the whole neighborhood.

We begged the HOA Board to let us paint it for nearly a decade but were always met with rejection. I think the Board enjoys watching my dad squirm. In all fairness, he's pretty funny when he squirms. Some days I'll whisper disgusting stuff into his ear just to see him writhe in overly dramatic irony, flailing his arms and kicking his legs haphazardly. It's objectively hilarious.

There is one thing I've always loved about our house: despite all the bickering and squabbling between my parents, you could walk through it and not catch a glimpse of their issues. We are the perfect WASPish family to any outsider.

And everything is in its place, all neat and tidy. Mom keeps it pristine. It has been her only job since before I was born. Dad worked. Mom took care of me and the house. They were both very good at their jobs.

Mom loves having everything in its place. She shivers and shakes when things are sloppy and messy. More than once we've been late to a movie because mom had to rewash a dish or spot clean the floor.

She takes pride in it, and so we all have pride in it. It's not much. Our house isn't big, but it has its charm. It is a very, very, very fine house.

I CAN'T EVEN

Posted by Delilah Clark × September 23 at 2:20 pm.

This morning I woke up to the sound of screaming. It wasn't the screaming of two people with nearly twenty years of history going at it. That happened on the regular.

No.

This was the blood-curdling scream of Janet Leigh as Anthony Perkins stabbed her repeatedly in the shower. It rivaled the greatest scream queens of the past fifty years. Outside of horror movies, I've never heard anything like it before. I hope I never do again.

I ran out into the hallway and saw my mom in the study, knelt over my father.

He wasn't moving.

He wasn't breathing.

It's really hard to write this.

I thought maybe putting it out there would help, but it's just making everything so much worse—maybe I should stop—no.

I already miscarried two stress babies and a third one is maturing in my stomach with every passing second.

"Mom. Mom? What happened?" I screamed as I ran into Dad's office and fell down next to her.

Dad was silent, stiff, and cold.

I shook him.

Calmly at first, then more violently with each moment of silence. I shook him so hard, I feared his neck would snap off. "Quit messing around!" I screamed at him.

I couldn't believe how limp and lifeless his body was. I once called Alex dead weight. I was wrong. Dead weight is so much heavier than you can imagine—it's indescribable. I swear my father was never that heavy. It's was like he gained a hundred pounds overnight.

Everything else is hazy. I only remember snippets, fragments.

Alex came and wrapped me in a blanket. The police asked questions. Paramedics zipped my father up.

Tea. Was there tea?

There must've been because there's a mug sitting next to me right now. I'm trying to get it all down before it fades, but it's already slipping away.

There's just one more thing I remember more clearly than anything in my life. I don't think I'll ever forget it.

The smell.

Not the smell of decaying flesh or blood. Nothing you would expect. It was the smell of feces. Nobody prepares you for it, but animals empty their bowels upon death. And in the end, we're just animals, right?

Seriously, the muscles that constrict your butt-hole and intestines relax, and everything falls out of you. Even if you squeeze every last piece of dookie out of your body, right before you die, some bits will still find their way onto the carpet.

And that smell is burned into my nostrils forever. My father, fastidious to a fault about so many things, and the last memory I have of him is the taste of crap in the back of my throat.

DEATH

Posted by Alex Dewitt × September 23 at 9:14 pm.

Death is deeply horrible and horrific. I've never personally experienced it before now. All my grandparents died before I was born, both my parents were only children, and neither had many friends in the States. I've never known anybody who died.

Now I do.

Delilah called me, sobbing. She didn't know what to do. She was blubbering through her words. Something about cops and Dad and dead.

I rushed over to her house. She was there, sitting outside, crying uncontrollably. Her mother sat next to her, shell-shocked and silent.

Cops filed in and out. They were everywhere.

Then I saw it. The stretcher. The body bag. They loaded it into a car and off they went. Tim lay motionless inside. Delilah and Kendra were left alone.

I sat with them. I cried with them. I was shell-shocked with them. I served them food. I poured them water. I forced them to eat.

I took Delilah up to bed and sat with her. I gave her tea. When she drifted off to sleep, I did the same with Kendra.

A good man is dead.

I hate death.

SITTING SHIVA

Posted by Delilah Clark × September 24 at 9:27 am.

Chunks of time are missing. Alex has been here, by my side, every step of the way. She's the only connection with reality I have left. She keeps pinching me to keep me awake.

That's the only way I know this isn't a dream. It's a living nightmare. Most of my time is spent staring at a wall in my living room doing something called "sitting shiva".

Basically, in Jewish tradition, immediately after a death, extended family sits in their deceased relative's house for a week and receives visitors. It's annoying and I want them all to leave. Only four more days left.

You're also supposed to bury the dead immediately, but Mom refused that little tidbit as a giant jab to grandma's side.

She had to be polite, for dad's sake. She would let them invade her house. There was nothing she could do about that, but her seething bitterness made her not schedule the funeral until after shiva was good and sat.

She hates dad's family, and they hate her.

My family's never been very religious. We've never been very family oriented, aside from the three of us. I'd never so much as spoken with a cousin on the phone until yesterday.

According to the scuttlebutt, my grandmother banished my dad from the family for marrying a Gentile or something like that.

At least that's what I've gathered from my seemingly endless conclave of previously unknown relations that have descended upon my peaceful house. The story seems to hold together because whenever my mother enters the room, my grandmother curses under her breath.

My poor mother. God love her. I don't believe she's said a word in days. She walks around in a trance—a waking daze.

Every once in a while, she'll enter the living room with a tray of food or some drinks, but otherwise she sits in the kitchen alone, smoking and drinking. I didn't know she'd ever smoked. I don't have the heart to tell her how much I hate it.

Meanwhile, I'm left glad-handing every jerk that walks through the door.

I'm as cordial as the next person, but after my dad dies, the last thing I want is to hang out with a bunch of people placating me and trying to make me feel better. So, the fact that our house has been brimming with guests for the past few days is extremely unwanted.

"His laugh was infectious," Mrs. Turnbell said. She never liked my father and frankly we never liked her either. As the head of the housing association, she cited my father for every minor infraction in the book. And now she was being nice to me? No thanks.

I told her Alex had pissed on her flowers and she stormed away in a huff. Alex overheard me and stormed off the other way. For one glorious moment, I was alone. But it didn't last long. Two seconds later a new murder of cackling crows descended upon me.

People like that came out of the woodwork—people that once had a grudge against my dad or a grudge against my family. People who thought they knew us, but all they'd done was live across the street for ten years without so much as a peep. His coworkers, some of them crying, others baking their feelings away. The fake sincerity and concern boiled my blood. By the end of the first day, I never wanted to see another living soul again. Now I'm numb to it. I just want it to be over.

Worst of all, I hate the conversations with total strangers.

"Your father was a great guy," Janie, his deskmate, said, as if that meant anything.

"He always kept his desk so neat," his boss, Edward, told me. Like that would make me feel better. As he spoke, I focused on the single piece of dandruff on his shoulder. How does one get a single piece of dandruff?

The only halfway-interesting person that came through was Jeremiah. He stopped by once, high as a kite. I think he saw the free food and thought it was a dinner party.

When he realized why we were gathered, the look of shock on his face was priceless. He ran out and returned with a gift for the house.

A parrot. A no joke parrot.

He said it helped him through his parents' death. He said he was sorry.

Jeremiah called my family "man" a lot, shook their hands one by one, and then hugged my grandmother. It was a lovely disaster. Then he left as mysteriously as he came, leaving me with a parrot.

Everything the parrot says is gibberish, except the word "death". It repeats the word death day and night.

I was already having fitful sleep, and the squawking through the night isn't helping matters.

So, I pawned it off on my cousin. Let it keep my pompous Aunt Patty up for rest of its godforsaken life.

SHIVA

Posted by Alex Dewitt × September 24 at 8:10 am.

Delilah hasn't eaten since her family came to town. It's just been a constant barrage of questions, comments, sidebars, and bitterness. I never knew people could come together for such a somber occasion and bring so much hate.

I don't have much family. I'm pretty much a lone wolf, except for the few times I see my parents when they breeze through town, and our summer trips out of the country.

Delilah's family is the only family I know. Tim was kind and funny, Kendra, caring and loving. Doting even.

Kendra and Tim told Delilah she could do anything, and they believed it. My mother never told me that. She told me I could do better, even when I won gold. "That's nice, dear," she said. "Only one?"

Kendra loves life though, really and truly. Delilah was a daddy's girl, for sure, but her mother often shopped with her, went to lunch with her, and even cuddled in bed with her while her father was away.

"You can do anything," was Kendra's motto. "Never stop believing," was Tim's motto. The best thing I could say about either of them is that they filled the world with joy.

I don't know how they did that, since they came from such cold and distant families. Families that seem to relish putting each other down.

Now everything has changed, and I have to be there for them, like they have for me. I'm over there a lot. I sleep when I can, but mostly I just sit around for moral support. I don't want them going off the deep end or doing anything crazy.

DAD'S CASE

Posted by Delilah Clark × September 25 at 7:48 pm.

When I returned home from school today, the detective handling my father's case was sitting at our dining room table, filling Mom in on the latest developments.

She was crying. She was always crying.

The rest of the family watched from the corners of their eyes, trying to be inconspicuous, but failing miserably. They're unbearable. I can't wait 'til I can kick them to the curb.

Two more days.

I sat down next to my mother and listened to the detective. I honestly couldn't believe the police department would let anybody so young detect anything, let alone head up a murder investigation.

If his badge didn't flash every time he turned the page on his notebook, I would swear that he was one of Jenny's friends pulling a cruel, fast one on us.

He explained to my mother that since she refused to consent to an autopsy, some piece of Jewish law mom doggedly agreed to for some reason, they had concluded their investigation.

I begged her to reconsider; told her that it could help the case, but she was unrelenting. She said she needed to "keep the peace", and that it "wouldn't do any good". It's stupid, but I have no power. I have no power to do anything.

The detective used a lot of fancy words and police jargon, but it was all to mask a simple conclusion. Without an autopsy, they determined that my father's death was a suicide.

I flipped out.

I KNOW that is a ridiculous accusation. My dad certainly didn't die of natural causes, but in my heart of hearts, I knew he hadn't committed suicide either. There's a lot I don't know, but I'm 100% positive on that one.

My dad didn't commit suicide, for sure. If he didn't die of natural causes, he was murdered. I don't care what anybody says. I don't care about some stupid report, or the facts of the case as they stand now. I only know one thing: my dad was murdered.

Suicide wasn't in his blood. He's never been the type to cut and run. I mean, Jesus Christ! I saw him hours before his death.

He was laughing at dinner and talking about how big they made pancakes in some stupid YouTube clip he watched.

After dinner he made us watch it, twice. That pancake really was something to behold. It fed 30 people.

That's not what a suicidal guy does, you know.

I will go to my grave knowing that my dad wasn't cowardly enough to commit suicide.

And as I watched the young detective walk out the door, I made a pact with myself: if it takes 'til my dying breath, I'll make him believe my dad was murdered, too.

BLACK

Posted by Delilah Clark × September 27 at 11:01 am.

I looked at myself in the mirror last night and hated everything about myself.

I didn't feel like a blonde.

 Blondes are chipper and nice. They wear pink and go to sporting events to support their friends.

They drink rape juice and flirt with boys in orange hats.

I don't want to do any of that.

Every strand of my hair belied who I was and how I felt.

So, I dyed it.

Black.

It looks great now.

I can't wait to see people's reactions.

FUNERAL

Posted by Delilah Clark × September 28 at 9:36 pm.

I stayed up for three days prepping my eulogy. Mom told me she was too worn out to speak at the funeral.

I had to do it.

I didn't know what to say.

I tried to tell her that, but she didn't listen. She wouldn't do it or couldn't do it. I didn't have the energy to argue. Instead, I locked myself in my room and wrote one draft after another.

They all sucked. Just for reference as to how SUCKY they were, here's my first draft.

"My dad was a cool dude. He did stuff with us and stuff. I really miss him. He didn't commit suicide. And he liked pancakes."

Hemingway once said all a first draft has to be is done, but even he would slap me for that one. Nothing I wrote after that was substantially better, either. At one point I plagiarized one of Knute Rockne's speeches word for word. The one from Rudy.

I literally wrote it word for word from memory, at one in the morning, after not sleeping for a week.

And I thought it was great for ten solid minutes.

Don't ask me what I was thinking or how that relates even a little bit to my dad's life—besides him being a lifelong Notre Dame fan. He made me watch Rudy three times a year like clockwork: the beginning of football season, the night before the championship game, and his birthday.

I arrived at the funeral home late, despite my mother waking me several times.

I couldn't drag myself out of bed, because of sleep deprivation and depression.

Most of the mourners were already seated by the time I got there. I walked down the aisle between a sea of black clothing and mournful faces. All eyes were on me.

My stress babies were kicking the closer I got to the front of the church. There were more people than I'd expected.

The priest cleared his throat then proceeded to drone on for two hours. I'd barely slept in nearly a week, and it was really hard not to nod off.

Let's face it—I did a couple times. I'm not ashamed to admit it. Alex told me at one point that I'd snored, only to be awoken by the uncomfortable jabbing of Mom's elbow in my side and a stern look from the priest.

But come on. That priest was way out of line. We don't go to church. My mom only hired that joker to piss off our Jewish family, which had overtaken our home for the past seven nights.

My dad had never even met this guy before, and they certainly never swapped stories. Yet the priest had no problem telling a quorum of strangers all about how my father lived. It was pathetic.

What do priests know about grief? They can't even have kids or a family. Their only loved ones are little boys—that was probably over the line, but I'm not deleting it.

Eventually, it was my turn to deliver the eulogy. Every eye was on me as I stepped up to my father's coffin. I looked over at his smiling corpse. He was always smiling. It was nice to see him smiling in death, too.

Then it dawned on me. I realized this would be the last time I would see him, ever. I teared up. My anxiety baby came to term. I named it Abed, after my favorite TV star.

I cleared my throat as best I as could and looked out at the audience, tears streaming down my face. I realized why public speaking was the number one fear in society; in fact, I don't think it's ranked highly enough. There needs to be a number higher than one.

"My father wasn't a great man. At least not in the way history describes great men. He didn't topple empires or destroy the Galactic Senate. He wasn't a scientist or a scholar. He didn't cure cancer or end violence among women. He was just a guy.

"A simple guy. I think he worked in finance or with loans or something. Frankly, I didn't ask, and he didn't tell. It didn't matter. That was the great thing about our relationship. We could be ourselves. There might have been a lot of complicated things about him, but it was simple between us. Because we are family. And I'll always remember that. I loved him."

I stopped a moment to gauge the audience. I think somebody coughed loudly, but otherwise the reaction was...non-existent. I bared my soul and all I could see were glazed looks coming back at me. I continued bitterly, resolute to win them over.

"What I cared about was that he never missed a softball game, back when I played softball, and he was always around on Friday for dinner. Man, he could eat. He ate more than men three times his size."

I chuckled. I couldn't help it. I think a couple other people nervously chuckled with me.

"And isn't that the mark of a man, not in how big his impact is on the world, but in how big his impact is on those that he cared for? If it is, then my dad was the greatest man in history."

I walked off stage, drenched in tears. The priest thanked me, turned, and slowly closed my father's coffin. I'll never forget that moment as long as I live.

And that was it.

Later that night, the extended family left without even a goodbye. I doubt I'll ever see them again.

If I do, it'll be too soon. I'm just glad they took that stupid parrot with them.

BURYING DELILAH'S DAD

Posted by Alex Dewitt × September 29 at 9:15 am.

I cried like I've never cried before. And I've cried a lot in my life.

I'm a bit of a crier.

I read early drafts of Delilah's speech and still cried. I laughed when she'd given me her first draft to edit. They were so bad I put a big X through the whole thing, and yet I still cried...even then.

Her second effort was better, and the third was better still. She stopped asking me after that. I think she wanted me to be surprised, but maybe she just didn't need any more criticism. I just wanted it to be good, you know? I didn't mean to offend her.

What she came up with was good. Not great, but she spoke from the heart. There's no need to be a perfect orator, or give a nation's moving speech. All that mattered was that you said your piece and made your peace.

When I walked up to her afterward, she yanked me aside and spoke in a whisper. "The investigation's over," she said. "They say it's a suicide. Don't worry, though. I'm going to give it to that fool tomorrow. My dad didn't commit suicide. There has to be some sort of conspiracy."

I tried to be supportive. But deep down, deep in the recesses of my soul, I believe the police. I don't believe in any conspiracy. I had to believe her, though. I can't cast her out. This will blow over. It's just the second stage of grief—anger. She'll move on in time.

TERRY

Posted by Delilah Clark × September 30 at 8:21 pm.

I had unfinished business with the fool that ran my father's case. Alex tried convincing me to just go home and forget about it at first, but she must've seen the fire in my eyes because she backed off that nonsense toot sweet.

So, after school, Alex and I took our bikes and stormed down to the police station.

See that's funny because it was storming pretty hard.

Seriously, I almost died a couple times on the trip.

Alex definitely came inches from eating it when a dump truck hydroplaned and almost wiped her out. Luckily it just drenched her, which is good 'cuz I'm not equipped to handle two tragedies in a week.

When we finally reached the police station, Alex was still soaking wet. She asked me to wait until she dried off, but I couldn't.

I just couldn't.

I was on a mission.

I bounded into the police station, leaving Alex in my dripping wet wake.

After weaving my way through the desk monkeys stapling and collating their lives away, I reached the wide, open space that movies usually call "the bull pen".

That makes it sound more romantic than in real life, but it's actually just a bunch of dudes jammed into desks no bigger than a standard crate. It's sweaty and greasy and reeks of rotten, fast food farts. Apparently nobody told them how to eat or groom themselves during police training.

Someone "lucky" enough to make detective would sit there. Crammed in a corner, downwind of the food and subsequent farts that came with it, was the detective assigned to my dad's case. He was being chewed out by a loud, burly man with a cookie duster.

Kind of looked like the comic book character one of my neighbors s obsessed with. John Jet, Don Draper? Dan Dash, that's it.

The burly one was laying into my detective pretty good. Spit was flying all over his face. It was glorious.

I'd learned a little about the sniveling, little kid who had the balls to claim my dad was a suicidal sissy.

His name is Terrence, the youngest detective I've ever seen—including on TV— basically the Doogie Houser of police work, and that was after failing the entrance exam three times, which would be impressive if it didn't reek of incompetence. He said it was nerves, but I know better. It's because he's a terrible police officer.

Finally, Dan Dash's less pleasant identical twin finished flinging sp t and walked away. I waited until he went back to work before I shouted, "Mornin' Terry!"

I could see his pen scratch, digging a deep groove into his paper at the sound of my voice. Maybe it was the fact I've been calling him every hour on the hour since he gave us the news. It's about all I can manage. It's gotten me through the last couple days. Having something to live for, even if it's small, is so important.

We chatted for a minute, but really all I wanted to hear was Terrence admitting his error. For him to admit he was an idiot and acknowledge that my father was murdered. That is NOT what happened, though.

After all the bike riding, this is verbatim what he said to me:

"It is still the opinion of this department that your father committec suicide. I tried to be diplomatic, but you've got to hear the truth. You've really got to let it sink in. This isn't healthy, so listen to me. Your father committed suicide. We investigated thoroughly and that's our unanimous conclusion."

It was the last straw on the pile of heaping garbage that was my week. Nobody tells me my father committed suicide. Not my mom, not Alex, certainly not some numbnuts detective!

POLICE

Posted by Alex Dewitt × October 2 at 11:14 am.

You probably shouldn't cause a scene at a police station. Seems like something every human being should know instinctively.

That's not something Delilah knew though.

I went with her the other day—through the muck, the rain, the teeming downpour—to the police station to talk with Terrence, the detective assigned to her dad's case.

Did I mention how hard it was raining, or how three trucks nearly ran me off the road? One hydroplaned an inch from my bike. It drenched me and gave me a series of mini heart attacks.

Delilah left me sopping wet at the entrance while she beelined ahead to make a jackass out of herself.

She was on a mission: a mission to convince Terrence her father didn't commit suicide. She'd called him fifty times so far this week and every time he gave the same answer,

"It was suicide."

What did she think would change if she went down there? Clearly, she thought her presence would lead to him having a change of heart, right there on the spot.

People don't work like that, though. They tend to harbor opinions for a while, especially when all the facts point in one, very specific direction. And all the facts point toward Tim committing suicide.

Delilah is nothing if not pigheaded, though.

She snapped when she heard him say suicide again. I don't know why she expected anything different in person. Maybe she figured her award-winning personality would save the day.

It didn't.

So, she went ape. Like seriously flipped her lid. Luckily, she's only ten pounds with no muscles. I held her down no problem and pulled her away before she could do anything monumentally stupid.

Good thing I was there, or she might've been arrested. She was gonna kill that dude. I saw it in her eyes.

She needs to chill out.

EIGHT DAYS

Posted by Delilah Clark × October 6 at 3:12 am.

It's been eight days since the funeral. After visiting that jerk detective, I've only left the house to go to school.

Have I even gone to school? I don't really remember.

I definitely haven't eaten.

I don't want to eat. Everything tastes terrible. I placate my mom and take the food to my room every now and then. Then I throw it out the window or flush it down the toilet. She doesn't really care, either. She's going through the motions just like I am.

We are living, breathing zombies. Please don't shoot me in the head, though. Or anywhere. I guess we're more like metaphorical zombies.

My brain hurts thinking about it. I'm going to bed.

NEW CLOTHES

Posted by Delilah Clark × October 7 at 7:04 pm.

I hate everything that I own.

Or I guess I should say I hated it, past tense.

Nothing I used to own exists anymore. It was all too cheery. Lots of pink, bold-colored cardigans and skimpy, spaghetti-strap, summer dresses. It blinded me, like looking directly into the sun. My makeup counter too. I had absolutely nothing that I could wear anymore.

So I burned it all.

I do love me a good, cleansing fire. Sometimes, during the winter I'd watch the flames dance in our fireplace for hours.

So yes. I threw everything into a heap, poured a gallon of gasoline on it all, threw a match and watched it light up the night sky. I even brought marshmallows to roast.

Today I wore the only things I own: black fishnet stockings from a Halloween costume, a faded, black shirt that said *Eat at Rosie's* my dad got me on our trip to Kansas, and a leather skirt I bought for Spirit Week last year.

My mom flipped out. She stuttered and stumbled, averted her eyes, handed me a wad of cash, and told me to go buy some new clothes. Whatever I wanted.

And I wanted black.

Black clothes to match my black hair and my black soul. Black boots. Black everything. For once in my life, Hot Topic was my friend. I didn't want to think about how to be perky, or pretty, or stylish. I just wanted everybody to leave me alone.

And nobody is left alone more than the Goths. People hate them; revile them even. Most importantly, Goths are left to their own devices, and that's exactly what I wanted.

REACTION

Posted by Delilah Clark × October 8 at 4:59 pm.

The sheeple's reaction was priceless. I was like a leper at school today.

I'm far from the most popular girl in school due to my propensity to use words like *propensity*, but Alex, being on the gymnastics team, titillated the imagination of every boy she came across. Something about being bendy really does it for Neanderthals.

Plus, she was super nice to everyone. So her popularity was through the roof. Because we are best friends, I go along for the ride. I've never been chummy with any of the popular crowd, thank God, but they'd acknowledged my existence and, on the whole, didn't seem to mind my proximity to them.

I was generally happy and cheery, or at least I used to be, so people enjoyed being around me. I rooted for all the right teams, said all the right things, and liked all the right stuff, so I blended into the hodgepodge of popularity.

But when I stepped into school this morning, dressed head to toe in black, that all changed. People went from waving at me and acknowledging my existence to running the other way when I approached, scared that some of my freak juice would rub off on them.

I'm not even sure they recognized me. I heard more than a few "Who is that girl?", "Is she new?" and "Check out the new freak (azoid).". Lots of people giggled or downright laughed. But they all left me alone. And that's what I wanted.

Everybody except one person.

Alex.

She just didn't seem to get the hint that I wanted to be left alone.

"Did you go shopping without me, Delilah? It's certainly an interesting look. Seriously, are we going to a costume party later? Please tell me we're going to a costume party later and I just missed the memo."

I told her there was no costume party, that this is how I dress—and I had burned everything else I owned.

Alex was incensed, flabbergasted. She could barely put two words together. "B...B...Burned." Finally, her lips and brain synched together, and it all clicked for her. "Burned! What about that cute scarf I got you last Christmas?"

It went up in flames, as did the matching pink Spirit Week shirts that were supposed to be flame retardant, and even the sweater I borrowed from her. I promised to get her another one—a better, black one.

I burned everything except my pink ALEX is #1 shirt. I keep that in a safe place.

GOTH

Posted by Alex Dewitt × October 8 at 7:11 pm.

Delilah only wears black now. I mean only black. Like black, black on a black background. It's literally the exact opposite of what she used to wear. Well, maybe not literally. She wasn't bride white every day before. But at least she had color. Now she has the absence of color.

Now her eyes are black. Her lips are black. Her hair is black. Her clothes are black. Her personality is just...black.

I get it, I guess. I mean she was so happy. So, so happy before. She would laugh and root and pick everybody up, because her parents were like that too.

Whenever I had a bad day, she put a big ole smile on my face, no problem. Whenever we had a bad day, Kendra and Tim would be right there with a joke and kind word.

But Tim wasn't happy, was he?

I mean he committed suicide. That's not something somebody does when they're happy; only when they're miserable. How do you synthesize that with life? How does anything seem happy? How does happiness look attractive to you?

It can't.

Yeah, it's a really childish thing to just burn all your clothes and become a Goth, but I mean we're just kids, right? I mean at the end of the day we're not adults. We're not equipped to handle something like that out of thin air, a complete change in our perception.

Tim was Delilah's hero. He could do anything: fix any problem, find any solution, and do it all with a smile. Now, that image is shattered. All she has is the past.

It's a horrible thing. It's a crappy realization. It's all around crappy, crappy bo bappy. I'm trying to be supportive. I'm trying to keep my head down, keep my spirits up, keep up with school—and Delilah's school (she barely comes any more)—and gymnastics. I'm going to do it all with a smile, to show her there's still positivity in the world, even if she makes fun of me for it.

SCHOOLWORK

Posted by Delilah Clark × October 10 at 11:49 pm.

I haven't done any school work in weeks.

Alex brings me more every night, but I haven't touched it.

I would estimate there's about forty hours of schoolwork on my desk, at least. Waste of time. They already told me I'm getting straight A's for the semester, perks of being a half orphan. So what's the point?

Now this might not be weird to any of you, but for me I used to do four to six hours of schoolwork a night. I would do school work for the fun, even if there wasn't a grade attached, to keep my skills sharp.

I remember actually caring about it. About taking pride in school. Something about Harvard. Is it sad that I just don't care about that at all?

My teachers have been really nice and supportive, when I've gone to class.

But I haven't been doing much of that. I barely take a backpack to school any more.

One thing I have been doing a lot is fighting. My temper is razor thin. Anytime anybody says anything to me that is even a little bit off, I smack them right across the face.

I'm not a proficient fighter, but I'm very good at getting in one good punch and running away. Nobody has fought back, except Gus, our resident bully. But that fatso is learning, too.

I've been to the principal's office more recently, than in all my years of schooling combined, squared, and then cubed. So I guess to the sixth power, then.

The principal turns a blind eye to my temper. The whole admin staff does. I can't get into trouble, it seems. Seriously, who do I have to garrote to get detention in this school?

Honestly, this "are you doing all right?" crap is wearing thin. My teachers, the other students, the principal—even Jenny's leaving me alone – are all talking to me in patronizing tones.

I want them to hate me as much as I hate them, which is passionately.

PSYCH WARD

Posted by Delilah Clark × October 15 at 6:27 pm.

Sorry it's been so long. I've been under 72-hour suicide watch in the psych ward. It's about as fun as watching paint dry. I'm sure you're worried reading that, but it's really no big deal.

I got curious about how somebody could commit suicide. I didn't understand it. I've been a little obsessed with suicide lately, truth be told.

I read about cases in the area, and around the country. I've read scientific journals and volunteered at the suicide hotline. But I still sat in bed at night wondering how somebody could take their own life.

All of my research has been pretty academic. Even the suicide hotline doesn't let you on the phone with somebody until you've taken a bunch of classes, so I spent my nights collating pamphlets.

You can't just have an academic experiment though. You need to get your hands dirty. You have to do some field testing.

So, I drank a bottle of drain cleaner.

Like I said, no big deal. I just wanted to see what it would feel like to die. I called poison control and they dispatched an ambulance before I took a sip. I was never in real danger.

Unfortunately, when you try to off yourself, the hospital forces you into the psych ward with a bunch of other wackos for "observation". Thankfully, I didn't meet Nurse Ratchet, or an Indian Chief, or any other cliché archetypes. I did meet a guy who swore he was Captain Crunch, but he didn't have any cereal, so that was disappointing.

In truth, most everybody I met was so drugged up it was hard to say what kind of people they were off the meds.

Some people fought through it though, like the Captain.

I met another guy who thought he was a goat. I watched him eat half a can before the orderlies took him away.

I was the only one not hopped up on medication or wearing a diaper. They just wanted to observe me to make sure I wouldn't try to off myself again.

Honestly though, I don't know what they would do if I wanted to do it again.

If they found me suicidal, would they just lock me up for the duration? Do they really think I couldn't find something to kill myself with in that place, if that's what I wanted to do?

I don't really care either way, because I'm not suicidal. I'm just curious.

And you know what they say about curiosity—it killed the cat. But satisfaction, that brought it back. Though I have to say there was very little satisfaction in it.

I didn't really learn anything. I just sort of convulsed a little bit, then went to bed. When I woke up, I was in an ambulance puking my guts out. It was, actually, very unsatisfactory. There has to be a real, comprehensive study on suicide from a practical standpoint. I'm going to find it.

All I got out of the whole experience was a week of my young life gone and a prescription for happy pills, which I have to take twice a day with food. But since I'm not really eating these days, that's going to be a hard pill to swallow. Get it?

I'm sure I'll figure something out.

Otherwise, things are okay. It's nice to have my own bed back.

KENDRA

Posted by Alex Dewitt × October 20 at 1:01 pm.

Delilah is MIA most of the time. She hasn't been to school. She hasn't come to any of my matches. I've won six more gold medals, three silver medals, and a bronze medal. I don't even care anymore.

She hasn't even talked to me besides the occasional "hey" in the hallway. I don't get it. I just want to help her. She thinks I'm too chipper, that I'm too hyper. SHE USED TO LOVE THAT ABOUT ME!

I took all her new stuff in stride: her moodiness, her Goth-iness, her meanness. I didn't even say one thing. Then she gets to be all jerky to me? That's not fair. It's just not.

It's not my fault she ended up under a suicide watch, yet she's blaming me like I called poison control and got her locked up or something. Hello, she called poison control on herself! Maybe look in the mirror one of these days!

And her poor mother. That woman has been through ell. She just lost her husband, and her daughter turned into a hospital freak show. I want to say she perseveres, but she's nearly faded into oblivion.

She can barely function. She burns food, half cleans rooms, lays catatonic all day, and stares off blankly into space.

She never worked outside of the house. Well, that's not necessarily true. At some point she could have worked. I've never known her to work, besides keep house. Now, she's got nothing: no income, no marketable skills. And she's got that big, empty house.

I don't even want to know what Delilah's hospital bills are costing her.

I go and see her every day. I help her cook and clean. Mostly, I'm just a talkative body in the house. The emptiness echoes when I'm not there.

There used to be warmth to Delilah's house. Chatter and laughter abounded and reverberated through every hallway.

Now, there is just deafening silence, accented with the whimper of a lonely, broken woman.

SUSIE

Posted by Delilah Clark × October 21 at 6:43 pm.

Since my mother can barely function, Aunt Susie, that's my mother's sister, is over at the house a lot, cooking and cleaning.

I love her, but she is the loudest person I've ever met. She has this way of inflecting after every other word, which grates on my nerves something fierce.

The years haven't been kind to Susie either. Overweight and permanently disabled, it's hard for her to move more than a few hundred yards without aggravating her leg problems, or her foot problems, or her back problems.

Of course, being overweight doesn't help, either.

It's a vicious cycle. It never ends.

Susie also isn't the easiest person with which to talk. She's abrasive and rude. She'll cut you off in a heartbeat with "I'm bored," or "That story sucks.".

I love her for that.

One of the few highlights of sitting shiva with that bunch of pompous, holier-than-thou jack-holes was the day Susie talked to my grandmother.

"Well I don't believe that we should have gun control laws in this country," my grandmother said. "After all, our forefathers didn't find the need for gun cont—"

Susie wouldn't even let her finish. Her voice was as much booming as it was grating. It was a high-pitched squeal that filled up every nook and cranny of a room.

"That's the dumbest thing I ever heard," Susie said. "You think because our forefathers had muskets that you should be allowed an AK-47? Well excuse me, but logic like that makes me want to move to Canada."

Then she hobbled out. Everybody was silent except for me. I rolled over, laughing hysterically.

COUNSELING

Posted by Delilah Clark × October 23 at 3:03 pm.

Courts mandated counseling for me if I want to stay out of the loony bin.

Did you know it's illegal to commit suicide?

Seriously, there are major repercussions if you want to die, but ironically, only if you live. I think it encourages people to do it right the second time, especially if counseling is the bull they've got to go through.

If there's one thing you should know about me, it's that I don't take kindly to people trying to analyze my mind. My mind is a series of free-floating radicals. Any attempt to make sense out of that is just stifling my creativity and I simply won't have it.

Unfortunately, I'm only sixteen and don't need juvie on my record, so I have to go.

But I don't have to like it, and I don't have to make it easy on the doctor. And if our first session is any indication, I won't.

I was amazed at how normal his office appeared. I don't know why I assumed otherwise, but I thought it would be full of mental cases in strait jackets. In actuality, everybody in the waiting room was pretty normal, on the outside at least.

At one point while we were waiting, my aunt whispered in my ear, "What you think is wrong with them two?" pointing to the only interracial couple across the room.

And when I say whisper, what I really mean is full volume for any normal human being. When the couple looked over with a scowl, she just smiled and waved.

"I'll bet it's marital problems," she said.

Soon after that the receptionist called me into the psychologist's office. His name is Dr. Bennett.

He doesn't really have any distinguishing features. He wears glasses. He is soft-spoken. He wore a turtleneck. From the pictures on his wall, he wears a lot of turtlenecks, and they were all hideous.

I sat on the sofa and noticed a marble bust of Sigmund Freud. For the first five minutes of the session, all I could do was look at it. I swore its eyes followed me wherever I went.

"Can we get started?" Bennett asked.

I returned him nothing, but silence. He didn't ask another question. He simply stared at me.

Not another word was spoken for the rest of the session, until a timer dinged, and he smiled.

"Our time is up. Until our next session." He held out his hand, but I breezed past it.

Before I got to the door, I turned to him. "Out of curiosity, how much did I just pay to sit in silence for an hour?"

Bennett perused his notes. "Sixty-five dollars."

$65.00!!! That's absurd!

I have to go to dozens of these sessions to avoid jail. Like an ungodly amount.

$65.00 x some ungodly amount = 65 ungodly amounts!

I can't believe we have to pay good money for that.

Maybe I should go into shrinking heads for a living. I love sitting in silence and judging people.

HALLOWEEN

Posted by Delilah Clark × October 31 at 11:46 pm.

Dad loved Halloween. He spent the entire month of October making sure every nook and cranny of our property properly freaked out the neighborhood children.

He used witches, coffins, zombies, strobe lights, cauldrons of blood, special lighting effects, and a ton of other stuff I don't even understand and never fully appreciated until this moment.

My favorite was always this special bucket of candy where a hand bursts out of the middle when someone reaches into it.

You know the one? It was nasty.

Kids walked up to the house, stuck their hands in, and this gnarled-up zombie hand popped up and scared the crap out of them. Kids ran away in terror by the bus load.

Dad laughed every time. He had a ferocious laugh.

This year, there was nothing. It's not even locked in the basement or some storage unit. My mom sold it at an estate sale last week.

She transitioned from emotional wreck who couldn't keep it together for three minutes before the funeral to a heartless, calculating—let's face it—jerk.

I think watching my dad get lowered into the ground formed a callous over her heart and mind; nothing could penetrate it, especially my emotional pleas not to sell my cherished memories of my dad, wholesale.

Some stuff I didn't mind seeing go, like the ugly Christmas sweater Dad wore without ever taking off from Thanksgiving to New Years.

Those Halloween decorations, though, were cherished memories I couldn't bear to part with, but mom insisted without remorse.

The day of the estate sale, I sat outside and watched all of my father's most treasured possessions get sold off like they were pieces of fruit at a farmer's market.

- The gold watch dad got as a twentieth anniversary gift from his company GroupThink ($8.99)
- An array of tailored suits ($100 OBO)
- This funky belt buckle he won at a carnival the year I was born ($0.99)
- The wedding album my mother kept neatly tucked under her bed since before I could remember (FREE).

Who would want a wedding album is beyond me, but sure enough some prick swiped it up before 9:30 that morning, proving the old adage, "If you give it away for free, some prick will swipe your memories and masturbate to them in the dark."

And yes, the Halloween decorations were there as well.

I tried to buy them with whatever money Alex and I could scrape together. My mother wouldn't tell me how much she wanted, so I offered every collar I had.

$239.

She wouldn't sell them to me. She wanted them gone from her life. She wanted them out of her house.

And she wouldn't budge.

I even tried to sneak some of my better-liked pieces back into the house and hid them stealthily around my room, but twenty minutes later they were back out on the lawn.

I had no choice but to cross my fingers and hope nobody would pick them up. After all, they carried terrible memories for most of the families on the block. I doubted their children wanted them.

For most of the day, I was right on the money. Families would walk through our yard and their young kids, heck even some of the teenagers and even a few of the adults, would steer clear of those horrific decorations, shivering and shaking with PTSD.

I thought I was home free.

But my hopes were dashed at 4:15 that afternoon.

Our estate sale was set to end at 4:30. We were packing up my dad's few remaining possessions when a large van pulled up. A fat Texan waddled out and right up to the decorations. "Oh good. They still he-ya," he bellowed. "How much for the whole lot, miss?"

I answered before she could, "The whole lot for $300."

He thought for a moment. "Hmmm, that's a bit high for this lot. Give ya $250."

I don't mess around. I wasn't up for a negotiation or a bargain.

I just wanted him gone. I wanted him to leave my property, and my dad's stuff, and never come back.

So, I upped him. To $400. Then $600. Then $800. Then $1,000.

Every word out of his mouth drove up the price higher and higher.

He was just a business man. He didn't want to give them a good home. He wanted them to create haunted houses around the country. He wanted to break them apart and split them up.

It was unacceptable. These were my dad's things!

I was winning. He turned away, ready to leave my things—my dad's things—when Mom shouted "$250. You can have it all for $250!"

I'd offered her $239 and she wouldn't budge—$239 to keep it in the family.

To give it to me, so I could remember something Dad loved. But she stood firm. She wouldn't even hear me when I begged her to let me have it for $250.

I would scrub toilets, do laundry, anything not to give it up. I even went up to $300.

Then $350!

She didn't budge. I watched him write the check and smile as he handed it to my mom.

I watched him grab a handful of Dad's things, his precious things.

My heart cracked in two.

No. It broke in two.

He asked if I could help him move all my dad's stuff into his van.

I snorted. "Do it yourself."

My mom scowled at me. We locked eyes.

She didn't care that she let every one of my dad's possessions leave. She didn't care that it wrecked me.

It wasn't about the money, or my feelings.

She wanted my dad to know, wherever he was, that his stuff wasn't welcome anymore; that his memory wasn't welcome in her life.

It was cold-blooded.

FREAKING OUT

Posted by Alex Dewitt × November 2 at 12:03 am.

I'm really, really trying to hold it together, but it's not easy. The one person I used to talk about everything with has thrown me to the wolves.

Do you know how hard it is to defend somebody that constantly throws you under the bus? Really, really hard.

I have a lot of friends. Or I had a lot of friends at least. Delilah insulted them all. I mean it's not like I was in love with any of them or anything, but they were cool, good people.

Plus, I have to see them every single day.

Delilah doesn't even come to school half the time, but I see them every single day. I see them at gymnastics, on the yearbook committee, and on the dance planning committee. Then, Delilah comes and insults them with one sentence.

Do you think they like that? Do you think they like me defending her?

They do not. They're all like "Aren't we friends too, Alex?" and "How could you let her say that to me, Alex?"

It's really hard.

I can't leave Delilah. She's like a sister to me. I can't just leave her alone in the world. But I can't keep cleaning up her messes, either. I have a life, a life I very much like.

A life with other friends that at least talk to me.

Delilah doesn't even talk to me anymore, like at all. Even when I go over to her house, she disappears into her room.

When we eat dinner, she grabs a plate and hides. She's completely shut herself down.

It's super boring and super offensive, but I'm trying to be supportive.

I'm trying to be there for her. I can't let her flip out. I can't abandon her. But damn, Delilah makes it hard. Like she's doing everything in her power to make me hate her, to be alone.

RUST BUCKET

Posted by Delilah Clark × November 10 at 8:02 am.

I catch glimpses of the most random memories.

Today I was fourteen, sucking on a lollipop. Dad stood in the driveway, diligently washing suds off George. He'd spent the better part of three hours waxing it. It never looked better.

"Could you love that stupid thing anymore?" I shouted between licks.

"Stupid?" he replied. "This, my dear, is your inheritance."

Little did he know how right those words would be. Or maybe they were prophetic. Once somebody dies, we tend to see everything they said as an omen of their impending doom.

It was all I had left of him. The only thing we didn't sell at that accursed estate sale.

Selling it off was too good for Dad's prized possession.

After Dad's death, my mother moved his car to the street and opened all the windows. She didn't put a tarp on it or anything. I think she hoped somebody would steal it. When nobody did, she got the next best thing. Nature is having its way with it.

The car has become a rust bucket.

The trees deposit their leaves on the seats, and water damage has warped the once-fine leather.

Dust settled on every crevice. Birds made nests in the glove box and poop all over the windshield.

It's amazing what nature can do in such a short time. We fight against it, but it always wins. If not while you're alive, then certainly once you're decaying in the ground.

OUTCAST

Posted by Alex Dewitt × November 15 at 4:13 pm.

I need Delilah to snap out of whatever's going on with her ASAP.

Seriously.

Girls at school are straight up making fun of me now. Delilah doesn't care, but this freak show crap is getting old. They torment me every single day. They used to be my friends.

Half the gymnastics team won't talk to me at all.

The other half actively root for me to hurt myself. Not that I ever would. Please. I'm a rock star. I run that team.

Ten gold medals and counting in four different events.

Eat that!

I haven't been invited to a party in over a month. Let that sink in. I'm a hot, teenage girl with a slammin' body that can bend any possible way you can imagine, and even scuzzy dudes won't invite me to parties.

What's going on with that?

I don't get invited to sleepovers, or even group hangs. I can't buy the eye of any guy at school, even the unpopular ones!

I beg Delilah to dress normal. To be normal.

She thinks when I tell her to dress normal it's because I'm embarrassed of her. I am, but I really just want her to be happy.

But I also want me to be happy. I can't be happy if I'm friggin' ostracized. It's not fair.

I need people. I need things. I need this to stop.

FORECLOSURE

Posted by Delilah Clark × November 17 at 10:18 pm.

Today sealed it! My mom is full on Loony Tunes.

Bonkers.

Off her rocker.

INSANE!!!!

I've ignored her recently. That's my bad.

That makes me a bad daughter, but I have enough sadness and junk going on in my own life. Sometimes, she's just a little much for me, you know.

But it's mostly because she's been a raging you-know-what more times than not, and when she's not raging, she just sits in the living room and stares at a wall.

Today I tried to bond with her for the first time in a long while. Just like the days we were happy.

I was ready.

I was pumped.

We were going to go get our hair done, get our nails done. Even though the thought of some ancient Korean lady touching me made my skin crawl.

I didn't mean that to sound racist. It's not because they are Korean. I mean they are Korean, but that's just who they are.

I don't want anybody touching my skin these days. I wish I was a prickly pear so that people would avoid touching me at all costs. Hugging people and shaking their hand at the funeral met my intimacy quota for at least five years. But I was going to do it—for my mom.

So, I came home from school to see my mother sitting on the living room couch peering over a stack of unpaid bills at the naked wall across from her. After a few seconds I heard it.

Sobbing.

My ears perked up. "Everything okay, Mom?"

My mom was really quite a beautiful woman once. And she really loved my dad once. There are pictures everywhere of them together, laughing and having a grand time.

But she's aged fifty years in the past two months. She always prided herself on her skin care regiment to prevent wrinkles, and now massive crow's-feet and mouth lines have grooved into her face and belied her age.

Her hair, usually smooth and straight, is tattered and wild. Stringy strands of gray weave through her once completely auburn tresses.

She's never colored it once in all these years either. That gray is all the result of my father's death and the oodles of stress it brought.

As I approached, she looked up at me, smiling faintly through her tears. I knew this woman for a moment.

Not as my mother.

As Kendra—devoted wife, sister, and daughter—the woman who married a man she adored and the one that found his body on that fateful morning. A real person.

That feeling of connection lasted only a moment, though, as my eye caught something in the periphery.

It was a letter. Innocuous as the others, except for the bright red stamp that read: FORECLOSURE NOTICE. "What is this?" I asked. "Are we going to lose the house?"

"Don't be silly," my mom replied in a daze. "What would give you that idea? Everything's fine."

I knew that wasn't true. The big red stamp said FORECLOSURE. They don't send those when everything's fine. "Tell me what happened."

She took a deep breath. I could tell whatever strength she had left zapped out of her in an instant.

Then she let fly.

She couldn't work and get mental disability payments, and even that won't kick in for at least another six months.

I had forgotten all about her being diagnosed with some sort of mental illness or another due to the stress of my dad's death.

Doctors told her not to work, and even if she could work, she couldn't keep it together for five minutes at a time.

Mom tried to remortgage the house again, but they wouldn't let her since she already has two equity loans and no breadwinner or collateral to justify a third. Add it all up and it's a storm of biblical proportions. We're right there in the eye, set to watch it all get destroyed.

I asked about Dad's life insurance, pension, and 401K. You know a l that stuff adults have to protect against all kinds of messed up stuff.

"Your father died penniless. Spent every dollar he ever made trying to keep up with the Joneses. All he had was his life insurance. But because he killed himself—"

Those words grate on me every time I hear them. We argued for a long time back and forth about it. I knew he didn't kill himself. Mom was adamant.

"Yes, he did, Delilah! I know that for a fact. Coward. And because that prick committed suicide, his life insurance won't pay out."

I finally understand the bitterness she feels for my father.

Honestly, I feel it, too. His selfish spending was going to bankrupt us.

I'd be pissed, too. The only saving grace that prevents me from going off the deep end with mom is that I truly believe he didn't commit suicide, and I know I'm right.

But it doesn't matter whether she believes my dad was murdered or committed suicide. The police believe it was suicide. So does the life insurance company. And she's left with nothing. Soon we'll lose what little we have left.

I held her for a good two hours as she wept.

Eventually, she had nothing left and fell asleep.

THE HANDBOOK

Posted by Delilah Clark × November 23 at 10:15 am.

Thanksgiving's coming up, and I'm finding it hard to find anything to be thankful for.

Not that I'm looking very hard.

But I finally found something.

I've been combing through the library, trying desperately to find any decent research on the psychological ramifications of somebody committing suicide.

I've had no luck for the longest time. Then I found it: stuck behind a reference binder, wedged in a forgotten corner, out of place and out of mind, it seemed the library had disavowed any knowledge of it. It is called *The Suicide Handbook*.

A small, thin book no more than fifty or so pages. The author's name had been scratched off of the cover and inside flap. All that remained of him was a signature and note: "Don't do anything stupid, J."

There was no library code, no ISBN, and the author had ripped out his information, and an Internet search yielded no results. It's as if the book had been wiped off the face of the earth.

Yet here it was in my hand. You only publish something if you want to be remembered. If you want to matter to somebody. I like to believe that eventually the author succeeded.

I'll be honest, the book is poorly spell-checked, and the grammar is terrible. But the visceral impact of the introduction captured me.

> *On January 19th, 2001, I began on a journey that*
> *lasted one full year. I was all kinds of messed up. I was*
> *bankrupt, on drugs, and alone, so terribly alone. So, I*
> *did what anybody with half a brain and a bottle of pills*
> *would do, once they realized they were worthless. I*

*took them all. I shook for three hours wondering what
would happen when I died, but I never did. I thought it
was a miracle, a sign from God. It wasn't. I was just an
idiot. I went to the emergency room and found out I
had tried to OD on multivitamins. I didn't know.
The label on the bottle was ripped off.
Over the next twelve months, I tried every way to kill
myself imaginable. And I failed every time. I took it as a
sign from God that I'm supposed to be alive. I hate him
for that. I'm not condoning what I've done. I just want
somebody to know. Anybody to know.*

The more I read, the more I had to read.

Once I finished the book for the second time, I realized the author was a genius.

The third time I thought the author was a moron.

By the fifth, the author might've been a god.

This is what's missing from my own research. It isn't enough to know the clinical mind-set of the suicidal. I'll have to run my own tests. But first I'll need to prep.

MOM

Posted by Alex Dewitt × November 25 at 11:23 pm.

Thanksgiving.

What do I have to be thankful for?

Not much.

Nothing has changed on the Delilah front. For the better, at least. My gymnastics coach calls me a distraction.

She said I was bad for morale.

Then kicked me off the team.

"Maybe next season," she told me. Twelve medals and kicked to the curb when Jenny healed up. Awesome.

Does she realize this is like my last season before I get all old and crusty? I can't wreck my body forever.

Mom told me she would pay for a private gym for Christmas, but I can't wait that long. Besides, that's not really the point. The point is this is getting old. Delilah might like to wallow, but it's ruining my life.

On the plus side, Mom is coming home for Christmas. Maybe Dad, too. It will be good to see them. I've barely talked to them in six months. I'm surprised they're coming home in the cold. Usually, they're only here in the sweltering heat.

I spend most of my time with Kendra. She's fallen into a deep shame spiral. It's hard to get her to open her mouth.

Bills are piling up. Foreclosure notices are piling up. I try to keep it organized. That's Delilah's job, but I've taken over.

I can only do so much, though. Kendra needs her daughter.

Something happened to rip Delilah and Kendra apart. I don't know what it is, but I know Kendra regrets it.

Things haven't been the same since Halloween. Neither of them will tell me what happened, but there is definitely a rift.

Delilah needs to get over it.

Delilah has a mother, a present mother. A suffering mother. I would die of happiness if my mother were half as present. I wish I had somebody like that.

I barely speak to my mother.

I was fine with it when I had friends—Delilah, Tim, Kendra—gymnastics, and a busy life to ease the pain. The only thing I have left is the dance committee.

And those girls all hate me.

THANKSGIVING

Posted by Delilah Clark × November 27 at 10:13 pm.

Mom wanted to have a can of old beans for Thanksgiving dinner, but Susie nixed that idea toot sweet.

She came over and made us a dry turkey dinner, rock-hard crescent rolls, and stuffing so salty it would kill all the slugs in town three times over.

"I don't care if you like it or not, I spent six hours cooking this for you," she said as we stared at our plates. "Now you're going to choke it down or I'll force feed it to you."

Susie comes over two, sometimes three times a day now. She cleans and makes sure we eat something.

When she isn't around, Alex fills in. Without them, we'd probably have withered away by now. I know my mother would have.

That's not to say Susie's gracious about it, or even pleasant. "I can't believe, with my sciatica, you're making me bend down to pick up your dirty socks," she told me once.

Another time I was out back, and I heard her scream. "How could you not have any cereal in this house? Do you know how much it costs me in gas to go to the store?"

It went on and on like that, day and night. Can't really blame her, I guess. We are a handful. But the truth is we just really have no reason to live or care. My father's death took everything out of us.

And Thanksgiving just brought it all into horrifying clarity.

We sat around the table, my aunt trying to start conversation, Mom and I sitting in silence, and Alex munching away.

I insisted on an empty place setting for my father, which my mother glared at throughout most of the meal. The conversation was SUPER tense.

"So, Delilah. You're wearing all black now, I see. What happened to your other clothes?"

"Burned them."

"Oh." She hesitated for a second. "Did you get a permit for an open fire?"

"Yeah, Susie," I replied snarkily. "That's how I spend my week, doing things by the book."

I didn't say another word for the rest of the meal. After that, even Susie shut up. In fact, I don't think anything else was said during the meal. The only noise was our chewing and the slight creak from our ancient chairs.

After the meal was over, we carted all the plates into the kitchen for cleanup.

My mother "accidentally" dropped my dad's place setting on the ground. The plate shattered into several pieces.

I saw her smirk. She really hated even the thought of dad.

It was the first time I'd seen even the smallest hint of satisfaction on her face in weeks.

GIVING THANKS

Posted by Alex Dewitt × November 28 at 5:31 pm.

Susie made the least delicious Thanksgiving meal I've ever had, followed by the tersest and tensest small talk in the history of family conversations. The stuffing was so salty; I nearly went blind.

Does she not realize salt affects gout? She complains about her gout all the time. You would think she might not want to make it any worse. Or maybe she does.

I can't complain about Susie, though. At least she tries. She busts her butt for that family, and neither of them appreciates it. I know I do.

We met a couple weeks ago and developed a schedule. When Susie can't check in on Delilah and Kendra, I do, and vice versa.

We turn off burners and cook dinners. We fold laundry and shop for them, so they don't die of starvation.

They would too. They are completely absent minded.

Mom sends me too much money for groceries every month, so I sp it her money in half and give half to Susie.

They don't eat much. I don't eat much. So, it works.

If there's one thing they should be thankful for, it's us. I know even with everything that's happened I'm thankful for them.

Even if it means eating my rock-hard, over-salted Thanksgiving meal in silence.

OPENLY WEEPING

Posted by Delilah Clark × November 29 at 3:41 pm.

My mother's been even more of a wreck than usual lately. She sobs nonstop, sits in the dark, speaks in whispered tones, and lays catatonic for hours at a time.

She often cries herself to sleep. I don't think she goes to bed anymore. I think she just cries until she's exhausted, takes a little catnap, then starts up again, and repeats that process about fifty times a day.

Susie and I tag team looking in on her, though it's usually Susie. Admittedly, it's always Susie. Maybe Alex too.

I don't remember.

I just know it's not me.

PITY

Posted by Delilah Clark × November 30 at 3:41 pm.

What about the way I look makes people think I want their pity?

Because I definitely don't.

I don't need it from the mailman. I don't need it from my terrible grand-family. I don't need it from my teachers or classmates. I definitely don't need it from my creepy next-door neighbor.

I definitely don't need him offering my mom a job. I mean why wou d he do that? You think we're doing so poorly you get to look down on us with your stock boy duckets, rolling in pennies?

I mean, do you really think my mom can work a steady job?

She can't even walk from one end of the house to the other without bursting into tears, how's she going to tell some numbnuts where the toilet paper is? Is that really the kind of person you want working in your store?

Or is it just somebody you want to keep around, so they can remind you that somebody's got it worse than you.

No thanks.

HANGING

Posted by Delilah Clark × December 2 at 1:27 am.

I swayed in the night air, dangling my feet above the ground. It was liberating, but scary. Very, very scary.

The Suicide Handbook has this to say about hanging yourself:

> *Most people only know what it's*
> *like to die the moment*
> *before they take their final breath.*
> *That must be why everyone's eyes bug*
> *out of their head. Pure shock.*
> *Not me though. I've died 27 times.*
> *Tonight, I tried to hang myself.*
> *I was nearly there. The bliss of nirvana.*
> *Never having to deal with the world again.*
> *There was a nagging feeling in my gut. Nausea.*
> *Queasy. I'd been hanging for 20 minutes or so.*
> *Slowly choking. Wondering*
> *what I'd done wrong this time.*
> *Suddenly the branch broke and I was on the*
> *ground. Another failed attempt.*

I don't know how J lasted 20 minutes. I barely lasted three minutes.

I gasped for air. My eyes bugged out of my head. I couldn't stand it. I took a razor blade out of my pocket and cut myself down from the oak tree in my backyard.

I didn't particularly like the choking sensation one gets with the rope around the neck.

I think I would have preferred it as it was done in the old days, when they strung you up in the town square, pressed a lever, and you snapped your neck as the door fell out from under you. Without that, it was like having a midget choke you out, which would have been a much cooler way to go.

Also, the heinous rope burn would make it impossible to wear anything but a turtleneck for the funeral, and frankly I don't look very good with my neck covered.

The creaking of the tree was really annoying too. I wouldn't want that to be the last sound I heard.

DANCE

Posted by Alex Dewitt × December 2 at 9:18 pm.

Thank you, Mr. Willis. Thank you very much.

Not only did you give me this terrible assignment to write my feelings in a stupid journal, you also made me the queen bee of the dance committee.

I know I begged for the honor for the past three months, but that was a *LIFETIME* ago.

It's amazing how priorities change. Right now, there's nothing I want more than to not have everybody hate me.

And guess what?

Becoming the chair might have been cool when I was killing it in the friend and gymnastics department, but not so much when I'm a social outcast.

I tried to fight with you, give it up, give it back, just fade into the background, but you wouldn't have that, huh?

No. You want me to plan the dance, a dance we haven't even really started fund-raising for yet, without adequate prep time, with girls that hate me, and still make it perfect?

You really do want the whole school to hate me, huh?

You really want me to fail.

You must, so you can hear about it in your stupid diary. I hope you like the show. I hope it gets you off. Just FYI, I hate you. You have brought nothing but misery into my life.

SHOWERS

Posted by Delilah Clark × December 3 at 11:13 am.

I've showered six times since last night.

Somehow, I still have tree sap all over me. It's in my hair and all over my body, no matter how hard I scrub. Some people might say it's psychosomatic because of the traumatic experience of almost dying, and the tree sap never really existed at all.

I know Dr. Bennett would say something like that. But psycho jerks are stupid.

I'm all sticky like I'd rolled around in maple syrup for an hour and never washed it off. Every time I sit down, I stick to the chair like it's covered in honey.

It sucks.

SHIT STAIN

Posted by Delilah Clark × December 4 at 8:43 pm.

After my shower tonight (yes, I still feel sticky), I left the bathroom and peered down the hallway toward my dad's wide-open study door.

Dad's shit stain was still there. No amount of scrubbing would ever clean it up.

At least it doesn't smell any more. Or maybe it does, and I've just grown accustomed to it. I don't know.

I hope that's not it.

LOLLIPOPS

Posted by Delilah Clark × December 5 at 3:43 pm.

I was eight.

I walked into the study as my dad typed on his computer. The wincow was open, and the oak tree gave the room a wonderful aroma. I loved that study. Nowhere else in the whole world made me feel safer.

"Daddy?" I asked.

My dad fumbled to turn off his computer monitor. He always did that when I walked into his study. A sign of respect, he said. He wanted to give me his full attention. Now I wonder if he was just looking up porn. But then it was sweet.

"I had a bad dream."

He patted his knees and I hopped up onto them. "We know what to do with bad dreams, right?"

I nodded. "We tell them that they should go away, because the light from our hearts makes them unable to hurt us. Will you lie with me until I fall asleep?"

"Sure, kiddo. Just let me finish here. Did you brush your teeth?"

I shook my head.

"So, you were going to bed without brushing your teeth, or you thought maybe you could sneak some treats from me first?"

I can tell you one thing from experience. You know all those lies we told as a child, the ones we thought were great? Yea, not so much. They are actua ly really terrible. Our parents saw right through them. Sometimes they'd placate us, but we're just not sophisticated enough to lie with any depth. I thought I was a ninja as a kid. I thought I'd come up with the greatest lies in the history of lies, but they were just—well, awful, honestly. They were awful.

Long story short, he was right. I hadn't had a bad dream. I just wanted one of the lollipops he kept hidden and locked in a drawer in his desk. For some reason they tasted better than any others on the planet. Probably because they were our little secret.

He smiled and reached into his file cabinet drawer. He pulled out a lollipop and handed it to me.

"Go to bed and I'll be right in. And don't tell your mother."

FILE CABINET

Posted by Delilah Clark × December 7 at 3:43 pm.

I was really craving a lollipop after last night's blog post. Like all day.

ALLLLLL day.

And not just any lollipop – the best tasting lollipop on the planet. The ones my dad used to give me.

My mouth watered for them. I knew there had to be some left in there.

So, I wandered into his study, running my fingers along every smooth surface I came across. I hadn't been in there since the incident, but I was hungry for the first time in months, and I wasn't about to turn a craving away.

Even if it meant stepping through my dad's office to get it.

He kept them in a locked file cabinet. My dad was very secretive. He could have gone pro, if there was a professional sport for hiders of things. There probably was, maybe in some remote village in Uzbekistan. He often hid things so well even he couldn't find them again.

Luckily, he had taught me how to pick locks.

Well, I should more accurately say, he unintentionally taught me how to pick locks. He'd seen some late-night infomercial on becoming an escape artist and bought the DVD. It was specifically geared toward the subtle art of picking locks. All you needed was three bobby pins and a can-do attitude, the box said.

Dad watched and watched that DVD, but nothing stuck. I think he lacked the manual dexterity with his stubby fingers. Once he threw it away, I swiped it from the trash can, and I studied it until I was a pro.

Since then, I've always kept six bobby pins in my hair, and made sure whatever haircut I got didn't make me look like a fool for wearing them.

It took me about sixteen seconds to open that file cabinet.

Once inside, I found my father's bag of lollipops and quickly popped two in my mouth.

They. Were. GLORIOUS.

Little tip: combine Lemon and Strawberry together and thank me later. It tastes just like strawberry lemonade.

I stuffed the bag under my arm and started to leave. But as I closed the cabinet drawer, I noticed a peculiar notebook sitting atop a stack of papers. What made it so peculiar was the inscription on the cover:

NOTHING TO LOOK AT HERE

Dad's scribbles filled every one of the interior pages. God it was boring. Only my father's secret diary could be something so droll.

Numbers, figures, spreadsheets, complex math problems, and a slew of other boring information filled every space.

Every page, that is except the last one.

On that page he wrote something else. I'm terrible at transcribing, but I'm not posting a photo of my dad's intimate thoughts.

Some Pretty Kick-butt Awesome Plans Before I Die
1. Fly a kite with my daughter.
2. Send a message in a bottle.
3. Eat my weight in chili.
4. Soar without a plane.
5. Have a tea party.
6. Catch the biggest fish in the lake.
7. Make the world's best sundae.
8. Win a classic car race.
9. Destroy something beautiful.

This was the last will and testament of a dead man, filled with all the things he wished he did in his life.

Honestly, it was pretty stupid stuff for the most part, and boring for the other, but it was nice to see dad had goals in life above caring for his car anc being a good provider.

TOOTH

Posted by Delilah Clark × December 8 at 6:19 am.

I did it!!!! I found a clue that could break this case wide open!

How you may ask?

Well it started as I was taking a catnap in Dad's study. Don't worry. I laid down a blanket and inched into the corner to make sure I was far away from the stain.

Being close to where he spent so much time helped me sleep. It was the first good sleep I'd gotten in a long time.

But it wasn't to last. I woke to the distinct creak of our broken staircase. It was Mom.

She would've flipped her lid if she saw me in the study. I don't know why, but she forbade me from ever setting foot in there after the incident.

She is SUPER anal about it for some reason. She doesn't care about anything else except for that.

I have no idea why. Maybe she doesn't want me opining about my father, maybe she doesn't want me walking over feces. I have no idea, but it is basically the one thing she has strictly enforced.

I was ready to run, but there wasn't time.

Mom was nearly up the stairs.

I ducked into the closet and pulled a blanket over my face.

Then, I waited.

In the darkness, I readjusted my hand.

It swiped across something.

Something peculiar.

I held it up to the slivers of light peeking through the slats in the closet.

It was a tooth.

A human tooth.

The killer's tooth.

I know it's weird to think about a tooth meaning something, but I know it does.

See, my dad had perfect teeth.

Seriously, like flawless. He flossed twice a day and brush religiously. His teeth glistened.

I know that's stupid, but there's no other way to say it. They were really bright, and he didn't have an over-bite, or under-bite, or anything. He could've been a mouth model for real. Flawless wouldn't be out of place in—well you get it, the man had nice teeth.

HELP

Posted by Delilah Clark × December 9 at 5:35 pm.

If I'm going to crack this case, I need help. Help in the form of the only person I can trust.

That meant waiting in anticipation at the bus stop until Alex crested over the hill.

It meant dealing with the Abercrombie skanks. It meant acting crazy by holding up a tooth and begging her to help me.

Alex shrieked when I showed her. "Ew. Ew. Ew. Ew. Ew. Where did you get that?"

I told her everything. She wasn't happy I was sleeping near a shit stain, but even less so that I found a tooth and took it into my possession. Least so that I was holding it up to her face before she had her morning coffee.

I begged for her help. I pleaded.

Alex just shook her head. "No, D. We're not going through this psycho stuff again. I thought you'd finally come to terms—"

I stopped her right there. I couldn't listen to that horse drivel.

Come to terms! I come to terms with nothing!

My mom's about to lose the house and I don't want to live on the streets.

This isn't about my crazy or lack of crazy; it's about pulling something out of thin air to get us another night or six in the house I've grown up in.

Because if we lose the house, we've got about enough savings to buy a very tattered cardboard box just south of town. I needed her.

I'm not too proud to admit I cried.

And she caved. Like she always did when I cried.

...on one condition.

That I help her plan the dance. She must be desperate to ask me.

Now there's nothing in the world I want to do less than plan this dance. Alex has been obsessed with it for months. Almost as obsessed as I am with my dad's case.

It is a huge honor for a sophomore to lead the committee. It was a huge pain for me to help her.

But I couldn't refuse, so I didn't. That just shows how desperate I am.

GROSS

Posted by Alex Dewitt × December 9 at 6:12 pm.

You can't put a gross tooth in somebody's hand. It's just not socially acceptable. I don't care if your dad died three months ago. I don't care if you think it's the key to cracking open the case. I don't care if it's made of gold.

Teeth are gross!

And she believes it's the key to solving her dad's "murder"? Let's be clear. Never in the history of history has a tooth broken any case open.

Ever.

Well maybe sometimes, but not this time.

Still, there's a determination in Delilah's eyes I haven't seen in a long time. A glimmer of hope. I am NOT going to snuff that out, no matter how dumb she sounds.

I mean she's got therapy, the whole Goth thing, and a bitter personality; if it gives her the slightest bit of salvation to imagine her dad didn't commit suicide, I'm fine with it. I will do literally anything to snap my friend out of her stupor.

Even if it means playing along with her banana-pants theories. It's not like I have anything else to do, except plan a dance from scratch!

Delilah promised to help though. She promised. She swore to me she would help.

Delilah's word is as good as a bond, or at least it used to be.

STREAMERS

Posted by Alex Dewitt × December 10 at 7:12 pm.

Well, Delilah's a grade A jerk rag.

Three people dropped out of the dance committee after Delilah's first meeting. She didn't waste any time before starting to insult their fat mamas. No wait. Only two were fat, the other was a whore.

And I mean it's true that Becky and Denise's mothers are lardos and Theresa's mom sleeps with anything that moves, but you just don't say that.

I literally don't have enough hands to do everything that needs to be done. Who's gonna do it all? Delilah?

Ha! Yeah right. I didn't have enough time, money, or resources to plan a dance with ten girls who WANTED to help me.

And now? I have no chance with her and the couple incompetent boobs who are left. We tried something simple today: pick a color for the streamers. Pink. Purple. Blue. Green. Red. Really simple choices, right?

Nope. World War VIII broke out when Delilah demanded black. "Black like my soul."

Screw her, right?

Nobody wants a dance like her soul. That would be a super depressing dance. Like the most depressing dance of all time. There would be nothing but sad oboes, dogs whining, and meat grinders sawing through bone.

Nobody wants to go to that party.

All I want is a nice dance, so people won't hate me. I tried three times to quit, and you wouldn't let me, would you, Mr. Willis?

This is gonna build character, huh?

I've got character coming out my ass! I do not want to go bald at seventeen. That's what I want. I've got plenty of time to "build character".

SEVENTH SESSION

Posted by Delilah Clark × December 11 at 11:37 pm.

I hate Bennett's waiting room. I hate the psychology magazines littered on every chair, table, and flat surface in the place. I hate the intense smell of incense. I smell like a hippie for two days after every appointment.

And I really hate it when I catch somebody staring at me. I can tell what they're thinking—it's the same thing I'm thinking about them. "What's wrong with you?"

Sometimes it's a little easier to guess what's wrong. One of his patients rubs her hands constantly and mutters to herself, twitching uncontrollably and cursing under her breath. It's pretty easy to tell she has Tourette syndrome.

Another one reeks like he took a bath in bourbon. Kind of obvious that guy's got a drinking problem.

But most of the time it's not so easy. They are soccer moms and working stiffs. They might suffer from depression or anxiety. But they might also have Multiple Personality Disorder or homicidal tendencies.

Who knows? Maybe they just need somebody to talk to, to listen to them since their family won't. Maybe they just want to get a break from their husbands, wives, parents, or children.

Today I was getting the stare down from a plump woman in a cat sweater. Cat hair clung to every inch of her clothing. She even wore cat earrings, too. This biddy loved her cats. I surmised she's an animal hoarder. She probably lived with 723 cats in her studio apartment.

Before I could confirm my hunch, Bennett's door opened and his latest victim—I mean patient—stepped out.

Surprisingly, it was a familiar face. One I'd seen around my house at least a half dozen times in the last few years. Tall, svelte, lanky, and impeccably dressed, I know him as my dad's boss, Edward.

There's one universal truth about psychologists' offices. You don't want to be recognized by anybody.

You don't want anyone to know you're a little crazy. It's shameful. It's also shameful that it's shameful—but that doesn't make the shame any easier when somebody knows you.

Edward was no different. Unlike his firm grip and solid eye contact when we spoke at the funeral, here he shied away from me, avoiding eye contact and giving the limpest of wrists to my outstretched hand.

"You are looking well, Delilah," he said. "GroupThink's not the same without your father, you know." He caught himself and stopped cold.

It took him five full minutes to unclench his bunghole and accept that I was doing alright. After all, only the sanest, most well-adjusted souls get court mandated therapy, right?

He stuttered and twitched for another five minutes before Bennett mercifully cut our conversation short.

He and Edward exchanged a funny look. Usually, Bennett's patients don't make eye contact with him, or if they do, it's broken off in seconds with a droopy head and contrite frown.

Not Edward. He stared down Bennett until he broke. I'd never seen any of his other patients break him down like that.

For all my hatred of his waiting room, I hate Bennett's office even more somehow. It's small and cramped.

He cheaped out on the smallest office in the building. That's probably why I can hear the AC unit and smell wafting dumpster crud every time I sit down. No insulation.

I wonder who else can hear me through the thin walls.

Of course, that wasn't even the worst of it. He crammed every inch of the office with junk: plaques, file cabinets, chairs and couches, a desk and computer, and gadgets packed to the ceiling. There is barely room to breathe, let alone sit comfortably. I wonder how somebody with claustrophobia could stand it for very long. Maybe that is part of the healing process.

I sat on a tiny futon, knees resting under my chin, in complete silence. We both knew the drill. I wasn't going to talk, and he wasn't going to ask me questions. It was a battle of wills. That was the plan at least.

He knows how to get under my skin, though. He rapped his pencil on the notepad. I hate that. It's like Chinese water torture to me.

"Think this is what Hell's like?" I asked half-heartedly.

"I think it would take a mighty caring devil to want to know what makes us tick."

"Well, he'd get a lot better sense of how to torture us if he could get inside our minds."

"So, you're saying that anybody trying to find out what's going on inside your head is trying to torture you?"

"Or get themselves off. So, tell me, Doctor. Which is it? Are you trying to torture me, or does sitting in that chair, judging me and everybody that walks through your door get you off?"

It threw him off kilter. I love to throw him off kilter. He sputtered about wanting to help all the people, including me.

I told him he just wanted to collect a phat paycheck. He stammered again.

It went on like that for forty minutes, until he stopped babbling and we sat in silence. He looked out the window, and I stared at the mockingly derisive Freud statue that adorned his desk.

I'd gotten under his skin good this time.

I had to be there. I had to sit with him for one hour. I didn't have to play his stupid games or answer his stupid questions, though.

FIGHT

Posted by Delilah Clark × December 12 at 1:11 pm.

Okay. Today officially toaded the wet sprocket. It started when I stepped into school AFTER the first bell rang, which meant I only had about six seconds to grab my books and get to class.

Of course, the second I slammed my locker closed the huge, lumbering brute that is Gus started picking on me. We all know Guses, even if you don't go to East Willow. He's your typical, bully jerk.

And I hate it when dumb jerks start with me. I really do.

 I mean I generally hate people, it's true, but at least if you leave me alone, I'll do the same. But when you say things like "Hey freak," as you wobble over to me, you're just asking for me to knock you out.

And that's exactly what he did. I tried to sidestep him, but he is horizontally as wide as a heavy-duty Mack truck.

Seriously, he would have to diet for a long time to be considered obese. In my younger days I might have cared about the glandular issue that caused him so much derision. Now I don't care one bit.

His fat ass disease doesn't make him any less of a moron.

The second time he said it, I politely smiled. I was perfectly pleasant when I responded to him. "Don't call me that. Let me through, Gus."

"Don't think so, freak!"

Then I snapped. "I said don't call me that! You're a fat, useless waste of a life!"

Gus slapped the books out of my hand. They scattered across the floor. He moved in closer. I could smell the rotten cheese curls hidden in the rolls of his fat and felt the flecks of chewed food that he spat when he spoke.

He didn't know who he was dealing with.

See, Gus is used to people backing away from him. He's always used his fat, ugly mug and deep, guttural voice to make the peons piss their pants.

Not me. I wasn't scared in the least. I stepped over the books and moved closer until I was inches from his fat, slobbering face.

"I called you a fat, useless waste of a life. Now back up off me."

Gus cocked back and swung as hard as he could. I ducked, and his meat hooks flew over my head. His punches were slow and predicable. The girth of his body prevented his arms from moving faster than really slow molasses.

When Gus cocked back and swung again, I stepped on his untied shoelace. His fat flaps tilted his center of mass and he careened backward. His feet slid on one of my books, his legs fell out from under him, and he landed ass first on the floor.

Gus screamed something as I moseyed off, but my internal chuckling drowned it out. Probably something about ruing the day or avenging his honor.

And at that point, I didn't want to even bother with class, so I left and bought a smoothie.

What's the point anyway?

GRRRRRARGAMEL!

Posted by Alex Dewitt × December 12 at 8:01 pm.

Delilah is ruining my life!!! She's so out of control the principal is calling **me** into her office to reprimand **me** for Delilah's actions.

"You need to control your friend in her time of need," she told me.

Really? Do you really think I can control what Delilah does? Well clearly you do, because you asked me. No. You flat out told me it was my job to make sure she comes to school and acts right. Are you going to pay me? No.

I already trek all of her books home every day and deliver her homework. I already catch all the heat for her actions.

Now I'm going to be the target of the school bully. I don't think he'll be any meaner than the people I used to call friends, though. At least he'll only hurt me physically; at least it will be over soon. At least he won't relish in my ostracization.

Get this, those jerk-wagons flat out stole money out of my cash box. We did a candy cane fundraiser. I bought all the canes with MY OWN MONEY, since the school had nothing to give.

Even though we sold over 500 canes, I didn't even make my money back. So either a) they ate the canes or b) they stole the money or c) both because they're little jack-weasels.

PRINCIPAL'S OFFICE

Posted by Delilah Clark × December 14 at 12:33 pm.

The principal called me into her office today. She sat behind her crappily made government-issued desk and I sat in the even crappier half-broken chair across from her.

She picked up the tiniest rake you've ever seen and combed through the Zen garden on her desk, calming herself.

"Eleven fights in three months," she said. "This is very upsetting. Because of your situation, I've been quite lenient—but no more, young lady. You have abused the system long enough."

"Fine. Give me a slap on the wrist and let me get back to class."

"I'm afraid this warrants more than just a slap on the wrist."

I didn't think she had the balls to send me home. I didn't think she'd ever suspend me.

Man, was I wrong.

HARVARD LETTER

Posted by Delilah Clark × December 14 at 7:28 pm.

When I got back into my room today, I saw a letter carefully placed on my computer. In the upper right corner of the letter was the Harvard seal.

My acceptance letter.

Or my rejection letter.

But let's be honest, it was an acceptance letter for sure. Nobody would reject the prissy, goody two shoes I used to be.

I remember a time when I would have been bursting at the seams to open that letter. To read my name and the congratulations. Jump for joy. Run around the house screaming. Jump into my dad's arms for a bear hu—

That wasn't me anymore. I couldn't care less.

This Delilah gets in fights, get suspended, and blows off school. Olc Delilah would hate New Delilah as much as New Delilah hates Old Delilah.

I did the only logical thing I could. I opened my window and tossed it onto the lawn.

It fluttered in the wind, away into oblivion.

It was sort of pretty in a way.

MESSAGE IN A BOTTLE

Posted by Delilah Clark × December 15 at 7:17 am.

Before my dad's death, if you asked me what happens when you die, I'd have probably said we just go into the ground and become worm food.

I liked the idea of God letting you into Heaven. I liked the idea of ghosts wandering the world until they completed whatever sort of thing they needed to accomplish before they could find peace, but I never really had any tangible or intangible desire to believe in a higher power.

Then my father died, and everything changed. I would be sitting in a room and feel a sudden chill—or hear the creaking of our broken floorboard.

I might have discounted it before, but now I want to believe—no, I need to believe—that my father is next to me during my darkest hours (which are all my hours).

I believe that he's here, with me, and he's got something to accomplish before he can rest.

Finding his murderer.

Hopefully then my dad might finally find some peace. Maybe then we would all finally find some peace.

But until then, I can bring him some pleasure by crossing something off his notebook list.

First up, sending off a message in a bottle.

So this morning, I woke up at the crack of dawn and headed out to the water. Our town sits on the mouth of a rather large river that runs down into a gulch, and finally into a canal, that dumps into the Pacific. I thought it would be the perfect place to send a message in a bottle.

Or if not the perfect place, at least the best place I could bike to in a day.

I stood bleary-eyed as I watched the sun come up over the hills. As you can probably tell by when I post these blogs, I don't get up early enough to watch a sunrise these days.

But I have to say, it was pretty awesome. The colors, the serenity, and the chirping of the birds were all pretty cool. Not worth missing sleep for, but cool nonetheless. I think my dad would have approved.

I opened my backpack and pulled out a bottle of Mr. Pibb. For some reason, it was my dad's favorite. I had to look for a while just to find a place that sold them in bottles.

It wasn't easy to find.

Then I sat down on a rock and scribbled out a note.

> *I hope this note finds you well, wherever you are.*
> *I live in a small town called East Willow.*
> *My father died recently, and one of his life goals was to*
> *send this message out into the ether.*
> *My dad wasn't a great man, but he was a good man.*
> *Honest, noble, and kind. The kind of man I hope you,*
> *or your sons, turn out to be.*
> *He loved, laughed, and was murdered by a callous*
> *jerk. Now, he's worm food, but I like to*
> *believe we all become so much more. I*
> *wish I spent more time with him. I wish I'd*
> *told him I loved him more. Don't make the*
> *same mistake. Hug your loved ones,*
> *be with them, and cherish them, because*
> *any day they may be taken away from you,*
> *and the hole they leave in your heart*
> *may never—will never—heal.*
> *If you're ever in America, look me up.*
> *My name is Delilah.*
> *Good-bye.*

I tested the bottle's tensile strength. I checked for any imperfections or holes where water might enter.

I found none.

When I was satisfied, I rolled up the letter and stuffed it inside. Then I sealed the bottle with a lighter and sent it adrift on the sea. I watched it disappear downriver before I opened my father's notebook and crossed it off his list.

At least one thing is crossed off your list, Dad.

Hopefully you can rest a little easier until I find your killer.

BUDGET

Posted by Alex Dewitt × December 15 at 11:12 am.

And four more people quit the dance committee.

Nobody liked Delilah's suggestion of "Rotten Maggot Flesh" as a theme, nor did they appreciate being told, "Piss off."

I'm down to two other people, a liability in Delilah, and myself.

Not to mention I'm already vastly over budget – not that there is any budget to speak of.

Every fundraising event I try loses money. Every time I call a vote to request more funds, I'm turned down.

The committee won't even let me grovel to the administration for help. The apathy is palpable with everybody left. They are literally the worst.

On top of that, the old dance committee members still have ideas of their own. They'll come up to me in packs and tell me I "better not screw it up" and give their suggestions:

- You know the gym would make a stellar night sky. Don't screw it up.
- People would just love a bigger dance floor than last year. Try not to mess that up.
- Don't forget to buy enough refreshments. I get real thirsty. I'd hate to faint of dehydration if you screwed it up.

And so on. I went to the theater department to try and see if they had any props or set dressings or anything, but my ex-friends already had them in their hip pockets. The theater nerds wouldn't lift a finger to help! GRRRRR!

I don't know if my un-dance committee promised them all blow jobs or what, but the theater department was wholly unhelpful!

Why is everybody so unhelpful???!

Why does nobody care but me!!!?

DROWNING

Posted by Delilah Clark × December 15 at 9:31 pm.

Here is what *The Suicide Handbook* says about drowning:

> *Drowning in cold water is supposed to be like going to*
> *sleep. For me, it was a nightmare.*
> *Shivering, freezing, I sat for a minute until my body*
> *adjusted to the cold. Then I sunk down under the*
> *water. The cold washed over me, but my lungs were on*
> *fire. Before I could pass out, my natural instincts*
> *kicked in. I couldn't fight them. I kicked and screamed*
> *until half the water was gone. I gasped for air. It was*
> *frightful.*

I performed my experiment much like J. I laid down in the tub until my body adjusted to the temperature. Once I was acclimated, I sunk below the water. I breathed out until there were no bubbles. And I waited. It didn't take long for the fire in my lungs to start. Soon, it was unbearable. My body thrashed around for a moment before I shot out of the water and gasped for precious air.

I wholeheartedly endorse every word J said.

On top of that I realized something.

If I died in this tub, my bowels would empty, and I would be sitting in feces-filled water until somebody found me. That is not a dignified way to die—my bowel excretion muddying the water and coating me in a fine mist of poop. They'd be scrubbing for days to get me ready for the casket.

No thank you.

CEMETERY

Posted by Delilah Clark × December 16 at 7:22 pm.

Before every session with Dr. Bennett, Susie drives me to the cemetery and tries to coerce me into visiting my father's grave.

I'd never been to his grave before; not since the funeral. It didn't seem important to me.

It's not like he's in there anyway. Maybe his body, but not him. If he's anywhere, he's by my side as I try to fulfill his last wishes, not hanging out in a cemetery.

But Susie always insists on driving to the cemetery anyway. The cemetery is a weird place full of weird people. There's this tall undertaker who seems a little too into the dead people's families. He's like overeager for them to buy something. His smile creeps me out.

There's a grave digger who has to be high on something because he moves slower than molasses. Sometimes I catch the funeral director yelling at him, as if that's going to motivate somebody that digs graves for a living to pick up the pace. Shocker, it never worked.

They're not weird in a bad way though. Some of them I could like if I didn't hate everybody on principle. There's this guy who is always reading comic books. He introduced himself to me one day as "Roscoe. Roscoe Fay." Like he's James Bond or something. He just sits under this tall, oak tree overlooking the cemetery and silently reads comics. I would watch him read sometimes, letting my eye catch a cool image every once and a while.

I would usually just sit there, looking out at the cemetery, until Susie gave up and drove us away. But today was different. Today, I felt a twinge in my stomach, a pang, not quite a stress baby, but maybe a stress zygote, or an unfertilized egg.

I needed to see his grave. I needed to talk to him.

Susie was ready to fight, but before she could open her big mouth, I pushed out of the door and walked over to his grave.

It was weird.

For all my research on death, I had no idea how to act in a cemetery. I saw a few people crying over graves and placing flowers on them as they rehashed their day.

That isn't me. I'm cried out.

His gravestone was simple and to the point.

Tim Clark. Devoted husband and father.

I read it over and over again. Have you ever noticed that any word you say over and over again sounds super weird? Just try saying *neck* two hundred times and tell me that's not a silly word by the end?

By the eight millionth silent loop, my dad's name sounded like an alien language. Maybe Zorgblopple, which I just made up.

"Hey, Dad," I finally said. "How are you doing? Probably not so bad, right? I mean worms might be eating your insides, but at least you can't feel how cold it is, right?"

I paused, waiting for a response from him. I felt like an idiot.

"It's been snowing here a lot. Remember when Mom went out of town for the weekend and it rained? You always said that God was crying because he missed her. I thought that was silly, but I always think about that when it rains or snows now."

I liked it. I liked it so much I skipped therapy and sat there most of the day. I really can't tell you how much better than therapy it is.

HANDOFF

Posted by Delilah Clark × December 17 at 9:38 pm.

I liked talking to my dad so much I went back again today, all by myself. I don't know what I thought I would find, maybe solace. Maybe a moment's peace from the constant hatred I have toward everything.

What I found was Jeremiah, being weird and arguing in my happy place.

I was halfway through the cemetery to Dad's grave when I recognized his shaggy hair. He was arguing with a man in a gray trench coat. The man vehemently shook his head, slammed a thick manila folder into Jeremiah's chest, and walked away briskly.

Jeremiah followed him, waving the folder maniacally through the air. "Just take it back!!! I don't want your goddamn money!"

Money? What was Jeremiah doing getting money at a cemetery? There had to be better places than holy ground to have a hand off.

My eyes followed helmet head. He wasn't particularly tall, but he had perfect hair. Not a single follicle out of place. I'll bet I could hit him with a baseball bat across the back of the head and he wouldn't even feel it.

I tracked Jeremiah back to his car. He threw the envelope into the passenger seat, flung the car into gear, and tore off.

He was pissed off something fierce.

I wonder what he was doing at the cemetery, and whose money he didn't want. I'd take it if he was just giving it away. We need it badly.

LETTER

Posted by Delilah Clark × December 18 at 9:28 am.

I came back from a shower this morning to find a crumpled-up letter on my bed. It was the one from Harvard I threw out of my window.

Susie or mom must have gone and recovered it.

That was nice of them. But what she doesn't know is that I don't care about that anymore.

I tried to get rid of it once and it found its way back.

This time I just crumpled it up and threw it in a forgotten corner of my room. Nobody would bother looking for it there, especially me.

MOM'S FLIGHT

Posted by Alex Dewitt × December 18 at 4:35 pm.

Mom's flight lands in a week. I'm so excited, I'm shaking.

I didn't think I would care so much about some stupid, little trip, but I really need to see my mom. This year started out so awesome and ended up so terrible.

Now every day is a slog. I don't eat. I don't sleep. Every waking moment either pulls me to school, dance prep, or caring for Delilah or Kendra. I'm a zombie.

The bags under my eyes won't fit into an overhead bin. They'd barely fit in checked baggage. I've aged years, decades even. I might be older than Mom now. She doesn't have a care in the world. I have all of them.

I need my mom to tell me it'll be all right. Because I don't believe that right now.

Lord knows Kendra's in no position to tell me. She doesn't even get out of bed most days. Delilah would just make it worse. All my other friends abandoned me.

I'm utterly alone. Going through the motions.

SCOPING

Posted by Delilah Clark × December 19 at 4:35 pm.

Jeremiah is a lonely guy. I've been watching him since the hand off. He's become my little, pet project.

I can't get that grave scene out of my mind. I mean why would he not want money?

It's crazy, right? Or am I crazy? Or both?

I've been snooping on him at home, but he's barely there. I don't blame him. That place reeks. Its odor gets worse every passing day.

Mostly I scope on him when he's at work. That dude steals a lot. Like a lot a lot. I watched him load up a cart with cereal in the middle of broad daylight.

I guess I don't blame him. I steal from Super Mart all the time too.

But he doesn't talk to anybody, ever. No friends at work. No girlfriend comes over to his house.

All he does is sit and watch TV, or smoke.

It's a little pathetic. And boring.

THE LIFE INSURANCE ADJUSTER

Posted by Delilah Clark × December 20 at 9:38 pm.

How much do I hate the cock-sucking, life insurance adjuster I just got home from seeing? TONS!!!!!!!!

Jesus Christ that sucked. I mean, I rode my bike all the way out there just to hear him screw me?!

Ahhhh!!!!!

I've been trying for months to get a meeting with this life insurance agent to plead my case for our money.

I haven't been even a little bit successful, but with my new evidence I pushed a little harder, and he finally caved.

He agreed to meet me for ten minutes. Ten whole minutes, like he was the pope or something.

Should have known by the smugness of his voice he wouldn't take me seriously!!!

It took Alex and me an hour to reach the adjuster's office. I'm not kidding. A freaking hour.

This guy's office is in the boondocks!

No, it's past the boondocks! The boondocks are a dot to his office!

But we finally got there. He let us in and we plopped down across from him. I told him that we had evidence that proved my dad was murdered.

"Present it then, darlin'. Let's have a look see." His lisp was strong and his voice wispy.

Present it, darlin'?! Who does he think he is? The queen of England?!

I pulled out the tooth and I handed it to him. He hands were thin to the point of gaunt, dainty, and demure.

"That tooth proves it. It proves my dad was murdered. Don't you see?"

He examined the tooth intently. He picked it up and placed it down. He cocked his head and squinted his eyes.

Then he picked it up again. Who needs to examine a tooth for more than a second?!

Every time he opened his mouth to speak, he would put his head down and examine the tooth.

"That's quite enough of that," he finally said.

He slid the tooth across his desk and picked up a bottle of hand sanitizer. I still don't understand what grosses people out so much about teeth.

I mean it's not like I pulled this out of my mouth. It had been on the ground for months and I picked it up. It's sanitary...ish. Nobody thinks picking up a quarter is gross, and it's got WAY more germs.

He shook his head and shivered. "That was...unpleasant," he said. "It's late and I want to go home to my stories."

Then he stood up without another word and shoved us out of his office.

And that was it.

We begged and pleaded for him to reconsider, but he told us that without a police report stating that my dad didn't kill himself, there was nothing he could do.

"I'm sorry. I really am. But pretty soon this matter will be put to bed forever and I'll never have to deal with you or your colorful mother ever again. Trust me, I'm counting the minutes."

He pushed us outside and locked the door. I heard the dead bolt click! I mean what were we gonna do? Honestly!

What a scumbag, getting off on screwing over a couple teenagers.

He talked a hard game, but when push came to shove, he was just another sniveling prick getting off on a position of miniscule power.

I know the type all too well. Their jobs are soul-crushing and pathetic. Their bosses are on them constantly. They are small and insignificant.

Basically, they suck at life. So, every time they get even a whiff of authority, they dive in head first, lording it over anybody they can.

There aren't bigger WASTES OF SPACE on the planet that those types of people!!!!!!!!!

AHHHH!!

Now what?!

THAT FRIGGIN' TOOTH

Posted by Alex Dewitt × December 20 at 9:13 pm.

Seriously, I'm going to take that tooth and throw it in a ravine or grind it up and dump it in a river.

Delilah begged and pleaded for me to come with her to talk to her dad's life insurance agent, present some new evidence.

I made her swear to me she had more than the tooth, and she did. She SWORE TO ME! What kind of sociopath lies to their best friend?

I've got 900 things to do for my mom's arrival tomorrow, and she knew that. Yet she still lied to me!

And I went along! She's my friend and I love her, so I went along. Against every bone in my body I went along! And she let me down again!

When we got there, she showed him that tooth and says that it's the reason her dad didn't kill himself.

That was all she had. I blew my whole evening for nothing!

Are you kidding me? How is showing somebody a tooth helping anything? I wouldn't give her bus money if she showed me a tooth!

What was he gonna say? "Well, this changes everything. Let me get that check for you now."

No. He wasn't. The only possible outcome was, "Ewww! That's disgusting!"

I don't have time for this stuff.

TERRY AND THE TOOTH

Posted by Delilah Clark × December 22 at 8:31 pm.

Maybe I'm crazy. Maybe I'm dumb. Maybe I'm on a quixotic quest with no possibility for a happy ending.

But I'm hoping some George Bailey miracle comes through and I get a Christmas miracle.

After tossing and turning for the last couple of nights with that crappy life insurance agent's words rattling around in my mind, I woke up this morning with an epiphany.

Why the heck would I deal with a life insurance agent, when the real problem is stupid TERRY and his STUPID FACE calling this case a suicide?

The insurance agent was VERY CLEAR. If I could prove my dad's death was a murder, then he'd have NO CHOICE but to give my mother her rightful money.

So, I went to see him after school; the wang detective who botched my dad's case.

"Still prefer the night shift, Terry?" I asked.

It was only five o'clock, but I could tell he had just got on the clock. I'd harassed him enough to know he tends to untuck his shirt and loosen his collar the longer he's been on the clock, and when I saw him, they were both immaculate.

"Still prefer the demon act, Delilah?" he grumbled through his teeth.

I slammed my hands on his desk. "Maybe I am a demon. Ever think of that?"

"Every hour on the hour. Now go away. Grown-ups are working."

I pulled out the tooth and placed it on his desk. He stared at it for a good few minutes. Then he poked it with a pencil. Why are people so mesmerized by a tooth? It's just a tooth!

"What is it?"

"Evidence."

"No. It's a tooth."

Then he summarily dismissed it, just like that jackass insurance agent. I mean how many small pricks can hold me down in one week?

It's friggin' Christmas for Christ's sake. Can't they see that?

I begged and pleaded with him to run DNA on the tooth.

I swore it would prove to be the killer's. I knew it in my bones. In my heart of hearts. I also knew I was a better detective than Terry.

All I wanted to do was have him run one stupid test, and I wasn't above using sympathy to do it, but he wasn't budging.

"There's no magic bullet, Delilah. There's no one-armed man. Deal with it. We investigated, and I can say with 100% certainty that your father's death was a suicide. Your obstinate attitude is endearing in its own way, it really is, but even I have limits. There were no signs of forced entry. All the windows and doors were locked. Your alarm wasn't triggered. It wasn't murder. Now go away."

And that was that. There was no more begging or pleading. He wouldn't hear another word about it. He just turned back to his work, ignoring my pleas.

Which SUCKED!!!!

But it's okay, because I left the tooth there for him.

I told him to think about it.

I know he'll do the right thing, because that's the kind of sucker he is. He'll watch the tooth until it eats him up inside.

And then he'll cave.

MOM

Posted by Alex Dewitt × December 25 at 3:14 am.

Mom never got on her flight. She called me from some resort and told me she couldn't make it. "I'm sorry, sweetie. Merry Christmas."

It was the one thing about this miserable year I was looking forward to and now I have nothing.

She shipped me presents, which I'm just going to donate to some homeless shelter.

I don't want them. I don't need them. I didn't even open them.

I guess I can't blame her. I didn't need her before now, and now that I do, how is she supposed to know how to act?

Delilah, Kendra, and Tim were my family. Now Tim is gone. Delilah has gone off the deep end. Kendra is catatonic. I would think she hated me if I didn't know she loved me.

I hate Delilah.

I hate her for making me need my family, my worthless family. My selfish, heartless, worthless family that couldn't give two craps about me.

I hate her for making me worry every minute of every day. I hate that I don't sleep.

Most of all, I hate Christmas and all its fake-ass cheer.

DEBT

Posted by Delilah Clark × December 25 at 8:31 pm.

> *There were no presents. There wasn't a tree.*
> *There was no cheer for my mother or me.*
> *My aunt tried to tempt us with cookies and milk*
> *But all we did, was sit and sulk.*

Yeah, I know that last part doesn't rhyme quite right, but you told me that poems don't have to rhyme, even if all the best ones do.

Mom was always in charge of presents.

Dad was in charge of the tree.

We would open presents, drink hot cocoa, listen to Christmas music too loud, and do all that other crap you see in Hallmark movies. Dad would wear his hideous sweaters and Mom would wear a big old smile. It was, objectively, wonderful.

Not this year. This year there was nothing. No gifts. No music. No tree. No Santa. No decorations. No...nothing.

Susie was going to come over and make us food, but her back acted up and she ended up laying on our couch all day, bemoaning her life.

Since there was no Christmas cheer in our house, I spent the day combing over our finances to see just how we got in such an awful situation. After all, my dad made good money and our house wasn't that expensive.

Then I looked at the credit card bill and saw the ridiculous stuff they blew money on. My dad bought Parisian Turtle Wax at $80 a bottle and tailored suits at $2,000 a pop.

My mother wasn't any better. She spent upwards of $1,500 a month on groceries for the three of us. I had no idea three people could go through that much food.

I guess it didn't help that my family doesn't do leftovers; anything on the table when dinner was over went right into the garbage can. Or that she drank booze like water. Keeping a well-stocked wine cellar and liquor cabinet is SUPER EXPENSIVE.

Mom's been drinking heavily every day for three months and we've barely made a dent in that thing.

Then you take the gym memberships, the yoga lessons, Zumba twice a week, along with scooping up every new gadget that hit the market, and it paints a picture of a family up to their eyeballs—over their eyeballs—in debt.

To their credit, my parents did try on several occasions to cut back.

I saw dips in the credit card bills where they tried to only spend $1000 on groceries for two, even three months at a time – as if that was a chore— but it's nearly impossible to spend LESS than what you once did, especially if you still have the means, and they would always bounce back into their old habits before long.

I remember my mother, a couple of months before my dad died, telling me that she kept a wad of emergency cash under her side of the bed, so she wouldn't have to be hassled by Dad for spending more money. The funny thing is, my Dad kept a similar slush fund to avoid Mom's nosiness. How much money do you think they wasted by not being honest with each other?

Just FYI, both those wads have long since dwindled into oblivion.

And now, we're in quite the predicament. The one thing I learned from all this snooping was that no amount of penny pinching is going to dig us out of this hole. We've got a massive amount of debt. The kind of debt only a huge windfall—like a fat life insurance policy—can wipe clean.

I really shouldn't tell you how much debt. It's really embarrassing—alright, fine-- $51,234!

That's crazy, right?!

I mean fifty thousand is a ton of debt. And I'm not even talking about the house either. And it's getting bigger every single day.

We couldn't pull ourselves out of that with Dad alive. There's no way we can pull out of that nose dive now.

ALEX

Posted by Delilah Clark × December 27 at 6:43 pm.

Alex's mom was supposed to come home on Christmas Eve, but she never got on the plane.

That's a terrible thing to do. I know she hides it well, but Alex misses her parents deeply.

Every time they are in town, she goes out of her way to be the perfect daughter.

Now more than ever, given my situation, she realizes how precious life can be. She tried to shake herself out of the misery of her parents' absence and actually cooked dinner for us on Christmas Eve. Alex cooking is sort of like seeing Bigfoot— a once in a lifetime experience.

When that didn't cheer her up, Alex didn't want anything to do with Christmas. She stayed at my house, on the floor. I think if she'd gone back home, she would have burned the place down.

Sometimes, I wouldn't trade my life with hers for all the money in the world. I may not have a father, but she doesn't have parents at all.

My dad always wanted me, but nobody wants her—except me, and even I'm on the fence some days.

PILLS

Posted by Delilah Clark × December 28 at 11:44 pm.

I sat on the floor. Pills were strewn everywhere. My breathing was labored. I closed my eyes, I was so tired. I couldn't remember the last time I'd had a good night's sleep. Actually, that's not true. I remember the last time: the day before my father died.

It was inviting to drift off to sleep forever, or even for ten minutes, but I couldn't. I really do want to live. I knew I couldn't call poison control though. Not after last time. I couldn't take being in a psych ward again. Luckily, I had a backup plan.

I'd pulled out a bottle of Ipecac and chugged it all down. I waited. My eyelids were heavy. They felt like thousand-pound weights had pulled them down. I was, however, able to keep them open until my stomach churned. And I vomited. Everything I ate for the past six weeks came pouring out of me.

I heaved into the trash can for at least ten minutes. Every time I thought I had nothing left inside me, more came up.

I wondered how much I could possibly have in my stomach. I cursed myself, Heaven, Hell, the country of Estonia for some reason, my dad, and Pillsbury for making delicious crescent rolls I couldn't stop eating. They didn't taste nearly as good coming up as they did going down.

When I was finally done and left whimpering on the floor, I dragged myself over to *The Suicide Handbook* and reread the chapter on pills. I already knew it by heart and could recite it in my sleep—with my eyes closed and both hands tied behind my back—in French. Well, maybe not in French.

> *Sleep. Isn't that what we really want?*
> *I know it's what I want, and I nearly found it tonight.*
> *I didn't use vitamins this time.*
> *I used my mother's old sleeping pills. I thought*
> *it was appropriate, since they killed her too.*

*I was nearly through when I heard a knock on the door. I
instinctively went to answer it. The brat next door. I
couldn't speak. I remember falling.
Then nothing. Next thing I knew, I
was in the hospital. I loved the feeling of surrender. It
was peaceful. So peaceful.*

And it was. It was peaceful.

GRAVE

Posted by Delilah Clark × December 29 at 11:09 pm.

I went to Dad's grave today. I brought him flowers.

We talked for a while.

He's still the only one that gets me.

JELLY BRACELETS

Posted by Delilah Clark × December 31 at 9:42 pm.

I'm going to take a second from my regularly scheduled programming to talk about an epidemic plaguing our schools—consider it a New Year's public service announcement—more so than rampant cheating, drug use, sleepiness from waking up early, or teachers packing heat or molesting children.

The #1 most terrible thing plaguing our schools is jelly bracelets.

Now I'm not a fashionista or a Maxxinista, or really any sort of -ista at all. What I am is a concerned citizen, and I'd like to explain what jelly bracelets are to all of you parents who might be reading. Of course, if you're actually reading this I would wonder why in God's name you haven't said anything to my mom yet, but that's another story.

See, you might think that jelly bracelets are cool and cute and harmless, but that's where you're wrong. That's what your children want you to think. In fact, there's an insidious game going on in schools all over the country that your daughters, the precious fruit of your loins, are playing with every guy in school.

Here's how you play: Girls wear jelly bracelets. Every color represents a different sex act that they're willing to perform. Seriously. Guys try to snap the bracelets. Whatever color bracelet they snap represents what sex act that girl has to perform on them. Again, seriously.

It's sort of replaced the idiocy of a rainbow party from a couple years ago. That's when girls all wore a different color lipstick, and all blew a guy until his cock looked like a rainbow. At least then the girls knew who they were going to blow. In this scenario, they have no idea.

Here's a quick rundown of what each of these colors mean. Now granted, the acts may be different where you are, but I promise you, the game is the same.

> **Yellow -** Light hugging. Pretty innocuous. If you have to wear a jelly bracelet, wear 500 yellow ones. You'll look like Big Bird, but at least you

won't be going down on a stranger.

Pink - Again, not too bad. You get a hickey. FYI, hickeys are stupid. I refuse to explain why. It should be obvious.

Orange – We're now starting to get a little more risqué. The chick is willing to kiss somebody of the OPPOSITE SEX.

Purple - The chick is willing to kiss somebody of EITHER sex.

Red - The chick will give a lap dance—I assume to either sex, but I have no data to back that up. All the girls I've seen get this one snapped have given a lap dance to a guy, and one teacher who was eventually arrested.

Green - Chick will perform ORAL SEX on a girl.

Clear - Snapper's choice. Anybody that snaps a clear and doesn't ask for sex is a pussy, though.

Blue - Oral sex to be performed on a guy. Basically, blow job.

Black - Bland ole MISSIONARY SEX! Oh, nothing that serious here—just a bunch of horny, underage kids banging each other, based on the tensile strength of a stupid piece of plastic.

White - Chick will flash you.

So, parents, stop your kids before it's too late. You don't want them arbitrarily having sex with Moses. Not to mention that jelly bracelets are ugly.

The more you know. Because Knowledge is Power!

NEW YEAR

Posted by Alex Dewitt × January 1 at 8:48 am.

Yay. A new year. I sat at home in the dark and fell asleep at 9:00 pm.

I'm so not excited about the New Year.

Mom called me up at 4:00 am to tell me the sunrise in St. Bart's was phenomenal and wish me a Happy New Year. She was drunk, happy drunk. She slurred her words and apologized again before Dad pulled her away giggling. "Sorry, honey. Gotta go. Love!"

Delilah came over. She didn't say much. She just laid on my couch. She laid on me. We talked like two strangers going through the motions. We have so little in common anymore.

I feel bad for Kendra, sitting home alone, so pumped full of pills and booze she can't feel.

Alone and asleep by seven at night.

If she even makes it to seven.

She sleeps like a cat, twenty hours a day. I highly doubt she'll land on her feet, though.

FISHING

Posted by Delilah Clark × January 7 at 11:29 pm.

I pulled a picture off the wall today: my father and I fishing for red snapper.

I usually hate looking at my smiling, perfect family. It's so wrong. I wish we had something that was more like how I feel. I'd give anything to see a picture of my dad looking bitter and greedy, instead of forcing a smile for the camera.

His face always contorted into this half-smile, half-constipated face whenever the camera pointed his way.

And that face led me to think about stuff, which led me to the stain that still decorates our study.

I was going to just throw the picture away, but I couldn't. It even sat in my wastebasket for a few hours before I fished it out again. See what I did there.

We'd gotten out onto the water really early, around 4:30 before the sun was even up. My dad always told me fish bite best in the morning. I don't know if that's true or not, but I believed it.

Kids will believe anything their parents say at that age. It's funny because that sort of stuff sticks with you, even when you grow up and all those "truths" become shattered by reality.

We were sitting on the dock. Dad had already cast his line, but I was having trouble putting a worm on the hook. They wriggled and squirmed out of my hand. A couple of them fell into the water. Grateful fish gobbled them up.

My dad was always patient with me. He rummaged through his tackle box and pulled out another worm. "Now, you take the worm and push it ontc the hook, like so."

My dad pushed the hook through the worm's body. It wriggled as it unsuccessfully tried to escape.

"Does it hurt?" I asked. "Does it hurt the worm? When you poke it through?"

My dad smiled at me, infinite patience he had. "No, it doesn't hurt."

Lies. All lies.

It hurt the worm like you wouldn't believe. There's no scenario where you stick a huge needle through something and it doesn't hurt. The worm drowned in a miserable, watery grave, with a hook sticking out of it. Best case scenario, a fish ends its miserable life quickly. Poor worm.

But as a kid, that was comforting.

Parent lies comfort children.

That must be how they become so good at it. They start lying with the little, innocuous ones about worms and fish, and work their way up to the big ones, until it eventually becomes second nature – until their whole world becomes a lie.

FIRST SUSPECT!

Posted by Delilah Clark × January 13 at 7:19 pm.

Oh my god! Oh my god! Oh my god! I knew snooping would pay off!

I think I finally have a suspect in my father's case, and it's our nasty next door neighbor.

I've been watching him since that hand off at the grave, slowing ingratiating myself with him, becoming friendly, getting to know him, and it finally paid off!

I went over to watch TV with him. We'd gotten to that level of chummy. I think I was chummier with him than with Alex.

His weirdness I got. Alex's was foreign to me.

About halfway through an episode of Judge Judy he smiled, and I caught something I'd never noticed before.

Jeremiah was missing a tooth, way in the back. Innocuous unless you were looking for it.

I'm turning my investigation up to 11. I need something harder if I'm going to turn him in to the authorities.

ARGUMENT

Posted by Delilah Clark × January 15 at 5:39 am.

Dad and Jeremiah had an argument before he died.

I remembered it in a dream. It woke me up in a bolt and I ran over to write it down.

It couldn't have been more than a month before his death.

I can't rightly recall what it was about, but I know it had been loud. The garage muffled the sound, but I know they were screaming about something.

Why can't I remember what it was about?

There's something they talk about on every cop show ever.

MEANS, MOTIVE, and OPPORTUNITY.

If I can figure out those three things, I can nail that sucker to the wall.

I already had one part of it: opportunity. Jeremiah had a key to my house for emergencies. I recalled something Terry said,

"There were no signs of forced entry."

Somebody with a key wouldn't need forced entry, would they?

No. They would already have it. Now I just need to figure out the rest of it. I mean having a fight is one thing, but was it worth killing over?

ABANDONED

Posted by Alex Dewitt × January 17 at 10:14 pm.

Shocker: Delilah abandoned me again.

She swore up and down she'd help me every day this week. We have to build these set pieces and cut out all the stars and stuff.

It's a two-person job, if I ever want to sleep again, that is.

I guess I'm never sleeping again.

All for some stupid boy.

Some stupid, gross, skeevy boy who lives next door. She's soooo sure Jeremiah killed her father. She should probably become obsessed with it. Oh wait, she already is.

Even when she graces me with her presence it's only to fill me in on the mundane details of her "stake out" before bolting again into the night. She leaves before making a single cut in the fabric or finishing a single poster.

I'm dying here!

So, I stay up all night, cutting hundreds of stars and moons and other stuff, one by one. Because the dance committee is now me. The other two members quit last week. I'm literally alone.

Whenever I bring this up, you just give me some worthless answer like, "You can do it. You can do anything. You're Alex!" or "Adversity builds character."

I don't need a pep talk. I need help. How about you get off your lazy butt and help me!?!

Aren't you, as dance committee advisor, going to be embarrassed if this dance sucks? No. Probably not. Because all the fault lies with me.

Did you know that Mom wired me money for private gymnastics lessons, but I can't even take them because of this stupid dance? Instead I'm using all her money to buy decorations and fund this thing myself.

I don't even think that's legal!

Did you know I'm out there doing fundraiser after fundraiser by myself, whenever I'm not calming my best friend—let's face it my only friend—off the deep end? Did you know that?

Of course not. And you don't care. Nobody cares.

They just want things done. They don't care who has to kill themselves to do it at this point. If I just say screw it and walk away, all the blame falls on my shoulders.

So, I have to keep going. I have to make it good.

I have to do it all. Alone.

INVESTIGATING JEREMIAH

Posted by Delilah Clark × January 28 at 11:12 pm.

I've been following Jeremiah around for the better part of three weeks. I've ditched school, I haven't eaten, and I've barely slept. I keep notes on everything that he does, and some things he doesn't do—like shower. I've compiled my notes, and this is what I've found.

1. His manager is asleep at the wheel. They must never do inventory at that Super Mart because Jeremiah takes nearly half their food home every night.
2. He needs to quit smoking. That boy goes through about a carton of cigarettes a day!
3. The guy who picks up our trash is a jerk. He caught me digging through Jeremiah's and threatened to call the police. Hey anus breath, you do know that trash isn't protected, right? You can do anything you want once somebody throws something in the trash can. I know, 'cuz I looked it up.

I'm about to die of boredom. I'm sick of waiting for him to mess up.

I have to move this needle and see if there's anything to Jeremiah. There's only one way to do it. It is time to turn my stake out into a break-in.

See how I did that with the out and in? It's always considered clever when you have to point out your wit, right?

JEREMIAH'S HOUSE

Posted by Delilah Clark × January 30th at 1:39 am.

I did it. I actually did it! I got into that scumbag's house!

I waited patiently in the dark, adorned in my new black jumpsuit.

When he slammed the front door and powered up the Yugo, I snuck in through his back door.

The great thing about the suburbs is that nobody locks their doors, like ever.

Last summer, Alex got plastered and walked in on her old biddy neighbors scissoring. It was nasty. Fat flaps and jowls everywhere.

Unfortunately, I didn't find one piece of tangible evidence.

I found nearly every flavor of Jolly Ranchers ever made, though. And I came across a sweet stash of lollipops, which I definitely stole for myself, but nothing incriminating. In fact, it didn't seem like Jeremiah kept anything interesting at all.

He doesn't even have a computer. The best I found was an old typewriter gathering dust in a forgotten bedroom.

The one thing that haunts me about his place is the stench of death. It permeated every membrane of the house—from the kitchen to the master bathroom.

I initially thought it was the mung beans sprouting in the sink, but this even overpowered them.

I tracked the smell down to the basement door. But before I could descend down the rickety stairs, I heard the front door creak. Jeremiah opened the door and slouched down on the couch.

"Mom. Dad. I'm home!" I barely made it out the back door before he got up and walked toward the fridge.

The weirdest part is that his parents have been dead for years.

MY NEW JOB

Posted by Delilah Clark × February 2nd at 8:23 pm.

Jeremiah offered me a job today. And I accepted.

Now I get to check him out AND get paid while doing it.

Sounds like a win-win, except for the working part.

We're just doing so poorly. I need to help any way I can. Mom's crying all the time. I have to sack up and bear the brunt of our financial burden.

So, you're looking at the newest menstrual-red vest wearing Super Mart employee in East Willow.

Yippee?

DNA

Posted by Delilah Clark × February 6 at 7:27 pm.

Alex and I have become regulars at the police station. Not as criminals though, we aren't like Tom the exhibitionist or Joe the public masturbator. We are here enough though to know all the players. Whenever we go to the police station, we are met with smiles and waves now, even when we cause a scene. Secretly, pissing off Terry so much and making his life miserable is one of the few things that brings me joy.

"Get that DNA yet?" I asked Terry, rounding the corner into the bull pen.

Terry opened a locked drawer on his desk and produced a Ziploc bag with the tooth sealed inside. "You mean this thing? They didn't say anything, Delilah. Because I didn't send it to them. Because it's a waste of time and you're being stupid."

I stared at him stunned. I literally couldn't get the words out. He wasn't going to help me. He wasn't going to lift a finger. I couldn't believe it.

I grabbed the tooth and hotfooted it out of the police station. People really, really, really hate the cops and cops don't understand why?

This is why.

FLYING A KITE

Posted by Delilah Clark × February 7 at 9:15 pm.

Have you flown a kite recently? I remember it being super easy, but it's not, at all. There are all sorts of questions you have to ask and steps to take.

1. **Where do you go to find a good kite?** It's not just a matter of heading to the local toy shop. I thought that would be enough, but the first two crappily constructed kites I got wouldn't fly two feet off the ground before they broke in half. I actually had to find a hobby shop. Did you know there are still hobby shops around? I sure didn't. Clearly this hobby shop, on the outskirts of downtown, didn't get the memo that people don't use hobby shops. Still, the owner was lovely. He took me to his back room where he had thirty different kites. Round, diamond, dragon, and basically any crazy shape you can think of. The options overwhelmed me, so I just picked a regular old kite—diamond with ribbon. Sturdy construction. Black, of course. Emblazoned with the Pink Floyd "Dark Side of the Moon" logo. METAL!!!

2. **How does it fly?** I was at the park and there were three-year-olds flying kites with no problems, but I couldn't get mine to stay in the air to save my life. I thought that once I bought a nice kite it would be easy, but I was wrong. I swear to God the laws of thermal dynamics, or gravity, or wind resistance, or something ceased to exist every time my kite lifted into the air. The only halfway acceptable time the kite worked was when I pedaled my bike REALLY HARD, pulling the kite behind me. Then it rose for about thirty seconds before is swan dove into a tree.

3. **Where is a good arborist when you need one?** Then there was the tree climbing. Holy moley that was an ordeal. When I was younger, so much younger than today, I could scale a tree in no time flat. My tiny, childhood arms swung from the branches and leaped between twigs as I rose higher and higher. But now that I'm at least sixty times bigger than before, I can't even get past the third branch up.

I had to call Alex for help. Her gymnastics background allowed her to flip and spin and get up that tree in about seven seconds flat. And wouldn't you know it? She flew that kite like a pro.

So, what have I learned?

> 1. Don't buy a kite.
> 2. If you must buy a kite, make it a nice one.
> 3. Be three years old so that air flow works for you.
> 4. Make sure you have a gymnast handy to get the kite out of the numerous trees in the park.

PS: Eventually my kite crashed into another tree and Alex refused to get it. So, if you want a free kite, there's probably one still stuck in a tree in the park by my house.

IDIOPIPHANY!

Posted by Alex Dewitt × February 8 at 6:14 pm.

If an epiphany is a sudden, intuitive understanding, what is a sudden stroke of stupidity?

I think it's an idiopiphany, and Delilah had one tonight.

She finally has some time for me. I guess she and Jeremiah had a stalker break-up.

Maybe not.

Maybe she's still scouting him at her new job at Super Mart (kudos to her for all the free Red Bulls and lollipops with her employee "discount"), but I haven't heard about it.

I don't really care.

She's actually come over every night this week to help me paint posters and cut stars. We got a lot of work done. We're a good team when she's actually trying. I could see she liked it too, even if she wouldn't admit it. She was laughing and even gossiped once or twice.

It felt like old times, for a little while. But old times don't last. Otherwise they would be new times.

Everything was going perfect. Then right in the middle of painting a big, glittery star, Delilah's head popped up. "I GOT IT! We have to go to the source. A dentist! Why didn't I think of it before? I have to go."

And she bolted out, leaving me to clean up her mess. It was a pretty star though, even if it was 1/1000th of the total I needed to fill the night sky.

Her idea to take a tooth to a dentist, on the other hand, was ghastly.

Idiopiphany, you're welcome, provided with examples. Let's get it into the dictionary, people!

DENTISTS = WORTHLESS

Posted by Delilah Clark × February 9 at 8:33 pm.

Well, adults officially suck. And adults that deal with teeth suck the worst!

We had a meeting with Thurman, my dad's best friend and dentist to the (non) stars. They'd been close since high school.

He had nice teeth.

I'm sure Thurman has other qualities too, but I don't really care what they are right now. The only memory that sticks with me is the one of him carrying my dad's coffin.

It's an image I'm not thrilled to remember.

In fact, I'd blocked him out entirely until my epiphany last night.

I was all excited when I handed him the tooth. If anybody knew about teeth, it was Thurman. And it anybody knew about my dad besides me and Mom, it was Thurman. So, it was a perfect marriage.

"Over the last couple months," I asked, "has anyone come in to get something like this fixed? Maybe somebody nefarious, or shifty. Somebody that maybe looked like he held a grudge."

"Okay, first off," he replied, "why would you assume that my practice deals in nefarious characters?"

It was an easy question to answer. East Willow is a small town. There are only two dentists within twenty miles. So nefarious or not, there's a fifty-fifty chance he would've gone to Thurman.

He tried to give me some crap about confidentiality, but that didn't fly. There are a lot of people I can't use that guilt card on any more. Thurman wasn't one of them.

So, he examined the tooth, because he obvi was going to, and it turned out it wasn't a tooth at all.

It was a crown.

"Luckily, they all have a serial number," he told me.

Why? After a huge theft a few years ago, they started stamping serial numbers on all their crowns, so they could track them. I have no idea who would steal dental crowns. Apparently, there's a black market for the material.

Is there a black market for everything? Who wants old teeth?

The serial number was miniscule. I'd written it off as a smudge, but sure enough when I squinted and cocked my head like a magic eye painting, there it was.

He slowly and deliberated typed every number into his database. His speed and dexterity was only matched by a ninety-year-old woman with carpal tunnel and bad eyesight who has never used a keyboard before.

Thurman's face dropped, and he shook his head profusely. Then, he dropped the bomb.

"I'm sorry. This is your dad's tooth."

My heart dropped. I asked him if he was sure. And he was. He showed me the record. Ten months ago, Thurman used that exact crown on my dad!

I was too stunned to answer him.

Even now I can barely speak.

It's not something that I like to admit, but that was pretty much the last piece of evidence, the last chance I had to clear my father's name. In months and months of searching, all I had was that tooth.

Looking back on it, it wasn't even a good clue. It was actually stupid. But it was all I had. And now I have nothing.

I need to stop thinking about this case for a while. Get it out of my head.

Maybe this isn't the last straw, but I don't see how I can stop us from losing the house now.

DENTISTS SUCK

Posted by Alex Dewitt × February 9 at 10:31 pm.

I don't agree with Delilah on many things these days, but on this we agree: DENTISTS SUCK.

They suck suck suckety suck suck.

We biked three hours, round trip, just for some stupid dentist to tell us it was Tim's tooth to begin with!!!!!

Why couldn't he tell us that over the phone? It would've saved me an evening and Delilah some heartbreak.

I just finished making fliers for the dance and two of the five big posters. I have 8,000 things to do and less than ninety days to do them all.

Of course, Delilah might not have even told him anything on the phone for all I know. Maybe she wanted to catch the dentist in some sort of lie.

She thinks she's some sort of Dan Dash or something.

She's not.

Dan Dash knows what he's doing. Delilah doesn't even know how to dress herself.

The more I think about it, the surer I am that Delilah wasted the whole day, not that dentist.

Dammit! I'm not gonna sleep tonight either way. I have too much to do. I don't even remember when the last time I slept was.

Awesome.

THE VOICE MAIL

Posted by Delilah Clark × February 12 at 9:43 pm.

I saw a blinking message on our answering machine today, which is weird. We never have messages; I don't even know why we have the thing.

I pressed the button and heard Bennett's voice.

> *"You missed your appointment today. In fact, you've missed every session for the past two weeks. I'm afraid this doesn't look good for your report. If you're not in my office tomorrow morning when my day starts, I'm afraid I'll have to call the asylum to be sure you're getting the proper care. Your choice: 9:30am in my office or sent to the asylum. BEEP!"*

I have had so much on my mind that I didn't even think about the doctor much. In fact, I'm not too concerned about going back to the asylum.

At least there I'd have a roof over my head.

But I have to be strong. I have to fight on—for my mother. And I can't well fight from behind the asylum walls.

SUPER MART

Posted by Delilah Clark × February 13 at 11:28 pm.

Days blend together in a smoothie of boredom.

There was school, then home.

After school, I'd knock on Jeremiah's door in my nasty, menstrual-red Super Mart vest twenty minutes before our shifts started.

He wouldn't answer the door for another ten minutes. Then he'd check the time, curse under his breath, and blow past me to his car. We'd get to work ten minutes after our shift began like clockwork.

I've been in training for two weeks now. It's dreadful. This guy who my dad knew came in the other day acting all teary-eyed when he saw me. He lived a couple of blocks away from us some years ago. Michael Fister. God, he loved movies. I mean like "leave your wife" level of love. If movies somehow could feel love, he would marry them.

He was blubbering and falling apart about how much he missed my dad. I almost burst out crying, until Jeremiah came up and told the guy to piss off. Actually, I think he said, "Go piss yourself." When I asked him why, why he would do that for me, all he said was "I didn't want you to be sad."

I must admit it's a little hard to believe that he's a cold-blooded kil er. In fact, he's even kind of charming in a morose way.

He's got a sick sense of humor. He likes to joke about death a lot. He just told me this one:

> Q: What's the difference between sex and death?
> A: Death you can do alone, and nobody laughs at you.

Funny, right?

And we are always playing games. Last Tuesday an old man was shuffling through the store, taking FOREVER to pick up enough soup to last him until next Christmas. Jeremiah racked up nearly $30 from other employees, betting on when he would die.

Another time, Jeremiah and I were kneeling in one of the aisles. He was showing me how to use the price gun on a row of salt.

"It's really easy—you just twirl the numbers until they match the right price, point and shoot," he said. "Why they give you a whole two hours to learn this is beyond me."

I smirked. "We can't all be as naturally brilliant as you."

"Well that's true." He flipped the numbers on the price gun for a moment, then shot at one of the salt bags. Instead of the $3.99 pricing we'd been told, the tags would read 58008.Or BOOBS.

Boys are so juvenile.

It was pretty funny though.

And that's how it's been every day, over and over.

The more he showed me about goofing off, the more I grew to like him. I don't mean *like* him—he might still be a psychopath—but the more I respected him.

Whether it was turning all the cereal boxes to point inward or stacking cans of lima beans to the ceiling in a single column so nobody could take one without crumpling them all to the ground, Jeremiah always has great ways to screw the management.

HELMET HEAD

Posted by Delilah Clark × February 15 at 12:40 am.

Just as I was crossing Jeremiah off my suspect list, he does something to perk up my radar again!

Jeremiah was smoking a cigarette during one of our many, many boredom breaks.

I don't smoke so I sucked on a lollipop. One of the perks of having a coworker who steals food is that I'm supplied in lollipops from now until the next decade.

He was pontificating about antimatter, or Superman, or something dealing with Bizzaro worlds, when he stopped dead, tracking someone across the parking lot.

It was the old Helmet Head. The one I'd seen with Jeremiah in the cemetery. He was still in the same suit I'd seen him in previously, except he was wearing a blue tie instead of a red one this time.

Jeremiah stomped out his cigarette. "I'll be right back."

He stormed off.

I tailed him between the two sedans illegally parked in handicapped spaces before I settled in the wheelbase of a minivan with a barking dog inside. Between its incessant yipping, I heard their conversation.

"Come on, man," Jeremiah shouted, "you've got to take 'em back."

"I'm sorry, son." the man replied. "Once you get the money, it's out of my hands."

"Then let me give you the money back! I still have it." I saw Jeremiah's feet as he struggled with the man, their legs entangling.

"Get off me. Get off me!" the man said, slapping him away. "I'm sorry for your difficulties, but other arrangements have already been made. Now good day."

The man walked away.

Jeremiah fell to his knees, crying. I scampered away before his eyes darted under the car.

I'm more confused now than ever.

This seems to be happening all the time recently. I don't like confusion, but it seems to be my natural state anymore.

TICKET SALES

Posted by Alex Dewitt × February 16 at 4:18 pm.

The un-dance committee destroyed all my work—again. I painstakirgly hung banners and posters advertising ticket sales.

It took me all afternoon and well into the evening to do it alone. It cnly took them 20 minutes to smear each poster with FREAK and DYKE in big, red letters.   It's an effort in futility.

Not enough people bought tickets to even justify a dance, yet you're making me throw one anyway.

We're supposed to get a DJ and food, hire security, pay overtime for cleaning crews, provide food and drink, and make sure everybody is safe for a whopping $137.

I couldn't even buy everybody nachos from Barry's with that amount of money. I can barely pay for the paper to make the signs people keep stealing for $137.

That balloon drop you wanted is definitely O-U-T.

I'm going out of my mind.

And what's worse, Delilah won't talk to me anymore. She's smitten with that jerk Jeremiah. She spends every waking second with him. She swears it's not love but come on. Every word out of her mouth is swooning.

He's a freak. She's a freak.

They deserve to be freaky together.

Which wouldn't be so bad, except that I still have to defend her to everybody. I have to make excuses for her missing class. I have to stick my neck out for her, and she reaps all the benefits.

Last night it got so bad I went over and spent the evening with Kendra. We cried and sat in silence. We watched *Jeopardy* and she helped me with one of my posters. It was terrible.

I never thought Kendra would be my best friend. Of course, I never thought Delilah would abandon me either. I guess time makes fools of us all, huh?

90 DAYS

Posted by Delilah Clark × February 18 at 9:32 am.

We got another foreclosure letter today. This one had 90 DAY NOTICE stamped across it.

This one was much more official. It had all sorts of really stern words.

And it gave a deadline.

May 18th.

If we don't pay everything we owe plus interest by May 18th, we're out of the house.

So, we'll be out of the house, because there's no way we can pay.

PARENTS

Posted by Delilah Clark × February 22 at 11:08 pm.

Escalation to the epitome of craziness happened today.

I don't so much mind the crazy, you see.

But that it keeps getting worse, and worse, and worse. That's what upsets me.

And then that new level of crazy becomes the new normal, and that new normal is then broken by even crazier bouts of crazy. I think, though, today I hit the wall.

The entropy. The moment when crazy can't get any crazier. Equilibrium.

Jeremiah just dropped me off after work. He bid me adieu and walked inside.

I watched him go, but I was uneasy about it.

Despite my desire to keep our weird relationship going, my inquisitive streak had burrowed deep inside my brain until it pulsed through my eyes and gave me a headache. I couldn't swallow it back anymore. It was giving me a stress quadruplet.

I had to know what was going on with old Helmet Head.

So, I ran up and banged on Jeremiah's door. He scurried and scampered inside, and the door eventually swung open.

"I haven't slept through the whole day again, right? I mean I did just drop you off. You can't possibly want to go back to that terrible store, right?"

I pushed my way inside. It somehow smelled even more like death than last time I was inside.

I ambled over to the couch and plopped myself down. Dirt and dust flung up and coated me in a fine mist of whatever disgusting crap Jeremiah had been doing for the past six months.

I carefully leaned back and stared at the picture above his television. It was a picture of him as a child with his mother and father on either side of him. And he was naked.

"They told me I could wear any suit I want, so I chose birthday."

They were an attractive family, if nondescript. If I had to draw the most normal-looking, boring parents in the world, Jeremiah's mom and dad would be model candidates. My eyes moved from them around the rest of the room. Along the mantle, all manner of food and supplies took up every nook and cranny.

"Are you a hoarder?" I asked. "Do you have a compulsion to keep this all in your house? Or are you building a bomb shelter? Come on, man, what's the deal?"

Jeremiah shrugged. "I don't know. Free stuff is free. I figure it's one of the perks of my job. If you count all this crap, I almost make enough to survive."

I figured his parents paid off the house ages ago and he was squatting for free, but apparently, they got a reverse mortgage before they died.

I looked it up when I got home. It's boring and I refuse to talk about it more, but you should look it up because it's a huge scam.

Why is the world always messing with old people? Probably because it's so friggin' easy.

This is the point in the story when stuff got weird.

Right at that moment was the point in my life when the weirdness meter spiked to eleven. He told me that if the house were paid off, he would be sitt ng pretty.

However, since he's got to pay a mortgage, he was stuck selling his thievings on eBay, taking odd jobs around town, or even— and here's where it gets nuts— selling his parents' grave plots.

Helmet Head was a grave broker. He goes around trying to get the best price for people's grave plots.

And Jeremiah sold his parent's USED grave plots to him.

That's right. That's what the stanky-ass smell coming from his basement was.

He showed me everything. My quadruplets came to term while we walked down the stairs. *Is this my death? Is this how it happens?*

When we reached the bottom of the steps, I saw two rotten, wooden boxes on the concrete floor of the unfinished basement.

He audibly sighed. "Those are my parents."

YOU READ THAT RIGHT. HIS PARENTS' COFFINS WERE IN HIS BASEMENT WITH THEM INSIDE!!!!!

There's literally no words to describe it, but Jeremiah sure tried. After a long drawn out explanation, this is what I learned:

- About a month ago, he was going to lose his house. The same jack-holes I've been dealing with hammered him as well. They refused to negotiate or help him in any way, which is their right as company representatives. It's just not cool of them.
- He looked through the local paper and saw an ad for the grave broker.
- He met with the guy, who told him that he only deals with unused graves.
- So, Jeremiah lied and told him that he's got two that would be perfect: his parents' graves.
- Jeremiah then DUG UP his parents' coffins and got the money.
- But he couldn't give the bank the money. It just felt wrong.
- He can't afford another plot, so he's been living with them ever since.
- Now, he's been trying to get the grave broker to take the money back, so he can put his parents back in the ground.
- But the grave broker had already sold the plots to a woman who needed to bury her sister and aunt after a horrific car accident took them both.
- So, he's stuck between a rock and a hard place.

It's a pretty horrifying and pitiful story. Sadly, one of the things that went through my brain is whether I could do something similar with my father.

But when Jeremiah told me it was all for $7,500, I shot that down. It just wasn't worth it.

THE WOODS

Posted by Delilah Clark × February 24 at 3:22 am.

It took most of last night and most of today, but we finally figured out what to do about Jeremiah's parents.

1. **Pull his parents out of the basement.** This is honestly the longest and most disgusting part of the process. I think he just slid the coffins down the basement stairs to get them in, but getting them up proved a challenge, especially since they were dilapidated and soaked through from the ground water. I can't tell you how many times they slid back down the basement stairs when we were over halfway up the stairs.
2. **Rent a U-Haul truck.** I have no idea what the people at U-Haul will say when they clean the truck and see disgusting goop from decaying bodies and smell death in the back, but I don't really care. I read the contract three times and am confident it won't cost Jeremiah any more money in cleaning costs.
3. **Drive the U-Haul truck to a secluded place in the woods.** We chose the place of his parents' third date. They were campers and loved the outdoors, so we took their bodies up to an overpass that overlooked the entire city, which I believe is where they did it for the first time. That freaked Jeremiah out so much he squirmed for a good ten minutes.
4. **Dig two graves and bury them again.** It was truly a lovely ceremony. We both cried: first he did, then I did, remembering my father, then he did again, then both of us. Jeremiah didn't say much, but he kissed the coffins before we lowered them into the ground. It was creepy yet perfect.
5. **Scrub the crap out of his house.** I originally suggested burning the mother to the ground, but Jeremiah apparently doesn't have the insurance for that, so it was nixed. We ended up spending the rest of the weekend scrubbing and disinfecting everything in his house with a hose and industrial strength cleaner. Even after all that though, the walls and carpet still reek of death.

It was surreal. I'd never dealt with death that up close and personal before. I mean my father did die, but the funeral home, grave digger, and mortician handled most of the up close and personal stuff. Aside from finding him that morning, I saw my dad at his most pristine. When I saw him, it was the person I knew. I remember him as he was.

For Jeremiah, it wasn't like that.

He saw his parents as rotting corpses, and that is rough. I mean you can only imagine the level of decomposition of two people who were laid to rest five years ago. It was, in a word, nasty.

One thing it did was bring into stark focus the idea of death, and what death means to me. I've struggled with it over the past several months. What happens after we die?

The simple answer is that I don't know. I hope our spirits are carried away to fulfill some other purpose, but I know this: our bodies go into the ground and rot.

Even if Dad was waiting for me to fulfill some purpose for him before he found peace, his body was rotting away.

And if that is all that happens to us—if we're nothing more than rotting flesh eventually—then there is some dignity and beauty in that.

We have but a fleeting moment to make an impression on the world, and eventually life will be over and all that will remain are the memories we made.

I don't know if I'm strong enough to believe that is all we are, though.

I don't know if I'm smart enough, or secure enough with myself, to believe that this is all there is.

I would much prefer to believe there is a grand scheme, and that once we die, I'll be able to see my father again.

There are so many things I wish I could do with him one last time, like going fishing or playing a round of Donkey Kong.

I want to hear him tell me that I look cute in my bright pink "Pink Floyd" shirt and ask me those stupid riddles one more time.

I also want my children (if I ever decide to push spawn of my own out of my lady bits one day) to see him when they die, and their kids, and their kids' kids and so on.

Believing we're just worm food—I just can't do that.

THE GRAVE BROKER

Posted by Delilah Clark × February 28 at 8:11 am.

If my weirdness meter keeps inching higher and higher, then tonight it broke completely. The glass busted and shattered everywhere.

I'm so sick of dead bodies, I can't even tell you.

After everything we had to put up with reburying Jeremiah's parents, we figured ole Helmet Head deserved a little payback.

We spent the better part of the last few nights drinking fifths of whiskey and figuring out how best to mess with him.

I thought we should put rotten eggs in his shoes, or stuff chicken in his grates and watching as he flipped out trying to find the smell.

Jeremiah, meanwhile, thought we should just beat him senseless with a sock of nickels and leave him for the dogs.

We agreed upon TPing his house. I think that's a valid middle ground.

Now, I admit it's a crazy thing to do, and very childish. But I'm kind of childish, as is Jeremiah.

I additionally concede there's not much originality in TPing somebcdy's house. But again, I'm not that original. There's a reason classics stand the test of time.

It took nearly two-thirds of the toilet paper Jeremiah had been stockpiling for the past year, but when the last strand of it went over the tree on Helmet Head's front yard, I knew we had made the right decision.

We went all out. We didn't just adorn the tree, but we encircled the house and the backyard. I cast it through an open window in the attic and even gct one roll down the chimney with a wicked bank shot.

Then I caught a whiff of something familiar. It smelled like Jeremiah's house. It smelled like Jeremiah's parents.

It smelled like death. Not as rank as Jeremiah's house, but the distinct whiff of decay.

I forced Jeremiah to boost me up onto the roof, so I could investigate. I shimmied across the gutter and pulled myself up. "Stay down there," I said. "Keep a look out."

Jeremiah looked up at me. "Are you kidding? First sign of trouble and I'm a ghost."

I ambled slowly over to the open attic window. The smell grew with the baby in the pit of my stomach. I named that one Raul Julia. It was at least a 12 pounder.

I crawled through the window and toward the rancid smell wafting toward me from the center of the room.

I inched forward, confident in what I would see, but hoping I was wrong. However, when I spun the chair around, it alleviated all doubt.

The grave broker sat with a bag over his head, pants covered in his own feces.

FLASHING IMAGE

Posted by Delilah Clark × February 28 at 8:11 am.

Images of my dad kept flashing through my brain all night.

My subconscious couldn't help dreaming of my dead dad any more than my conscious could help flashing back to that horrible morning.

Their deaths. Their deaths were so similar. No forced entry. Dead in their offices. Their bodies limp. They both looked almost peaceful.

I almost felt bad for the guy. Jerk as he was, I'm sure he had a family—I mean not living with him, obviously, or they would have had to of been deaf, dumb, blind, and anosmic to miss him dying—or at least somebody who cared for him.

I wiped Jeremiah off my list of suspects at least. There's no way he would have been dumb enough to drive me to the scene of the crime and help boost me onto the roof if he'd been the killer.

Which probably means he didn't kill my dad either.

MOSES

Posted by Alex Dewitt × March 3 at 7:14 pm.

Two months.

In two months, we pull back the curtain on this debacle of a dance. I've been able to cobble together an iPad, 400 songs on shuffle, and a few bottles of Shasta.

And I'm still over budget.

I've had to cut everything. The starry night sky theme. The magical entrance balloons. All of it is ruined. All of it is cut. Everybody's gonna hate me.

Except for Moses. Moses is cool with me. I've always thought him as a freak—a wallflower with no personality.

But he's got a big heart. He saw people pull down another barrage of my posters. He heard them call me a dyke. It was too much for him.

He found me crying and made sure I was all right—and asked if I needed help.

I hate to admit it, but my first thought was, have I fallen so low that even Moses pities me? But I have. I really, really have.

And Moses was good. He was quick. He had nimble hands. He was nice. He showed up on time and stayed late.

Weirdly, once he started helping me, the heckling stopped.

There must be some code that once you've fallen to Moses' level, you don't even warrant consideration. Everybody has written me off as a fail.

ANOTHER FUNERAL

Posted by Delilah Clark × March 4 at 11:31 pm.

Jeremiah took me to Helmet Head's funeral.

I know it's stupid, but I felt guilty darting out of that house without so much as a goodbye.

I'd seen something personal. Deeply personal. I'd connected with him in a way you don't normally connect to somebody; through their death.

Before they were placed in a casket, and gussied up, and made to look human again, and their eyes closed. You got to look into their soulless dead eyes.

It's very powerful.

It was a lovely ceremony, bereft of people. While dozens of people came to send my father into oblivion, nobody came for him. It was really quite sad.

Frank. His name was Frank.

In death, you have a name.

His name was Frank.

PINS AND NEEDLES

Posted by Delilah Clark × March 5 at 10:22 pm.

The police haven't interviewed us about what happened to Frank yet. I'm on pins and needles waiting.

I know my fingerprints were all over that room.

Not just on the chair and the roof, but also on the toilet paper that was all over the yard.

They haven't interviewed Jeremiah, either.

Maybe they won't come.

Maybe they think it's a suicide.

It wouldn't be the first time.

—J—

Posted by Delilah Clark × March 6 at 8:24 pm.

Jack Daniels is a truth teller, my friend!

A true miracle worker.

Then last night things got weird. I went over to Jeremiah's house like I always do, and helped him kill a fifth of Jack, like I always do.

We were joking and laughing. We were having a good time. Then, things turned serious.

"A few years ago, after my parents died, everything hit the fan for me at once. I was messed up. I didn't want to live any more. I tried to kill myself, like fifty times. I wrote a book about it even. So stupid." he told me, in that slow, slurred speech only drunks and stroke victims manage.

That's right. Soak it in for a second.

JEREMIAH

is

J!

He wrote the book that I've been obsessing about for the past FOREVER.

It turned Jeremiah, my gross neighbor, who was kind of kooky and fun to talk to, into a poet.

In retrospect, I'm an idiot. I totally knew he broke all the bones in his body after a car accident, but I didn't put two and two together. Mostly because I didn't care.

I'm not proud of what I did next. Well, I kind of am.

I kissed him.

I couldn't help it. Every ounce of my pent-up teen angst took itself out on Jeremiah's surprisingly hard and callused lips.

He resisted at first, but alcohol plus attractive, nubile girl begging for it could turn the most righteous man, and Jeremiah certainly wasn't that.

It was glorious.

For a moment, we intertwined. I forgot about all my problems...and then I puked.

All over him. It killed the mood.

AHHHHHHHHHHHHHH!!

Posted by Delilah Clark × March 8 at 9:57 pm.

Well just as soon as something good happens to me, it all gets taken away.

I can't believe this! I can't believe Jeremiah. I can't believe my luck. And I can't believe ANYTHING!

Get this. Jeremiah pretty much told me he killed my dad. Or if not, he had some pretty solid motivation. Here's how it went down.

I brought him over a new Van Halen t-shirt to make up for the one I puked all over.

When he opened the door, it looked like he'd been sucked dry by a vampire.

Before I could say anything, Jeremiah pulled me inside. First, I thought he wanted to make out again, but then he spoke. "I have to tell you something. It's about your father."

Then he let it spill. He told me all about the fight he and my dad had. The one I couldn't remember for so long.

Dad found Jeremiah's parents. He'd seen Jeremiah drag them into the basement.

He told Jeremiah to get rid of them or he'd report him to the police. That even if he got rid of them, he might report Jeremiah anyway. That he'd never liked Jeremiah.

A week later my dad was dead.

Can you believe that? Who says stuff like that?!? I can't believe I made out with a murdering scumbag!

HIT AND RUN

Posted by Delilah Clark × March 9 at 1:03 am.

I felt like I'd been hit by a car.

I'm not sure whether I overreacted about Jeremiah, but it doesn't make my feelings any different.

Suddenly, I can't trust him. This person I thought I knew. Somebody who I'd blown off my friend to hang out with. Somebody I thought I cared about. How could I get it so wrong? Why hadn't I stuck with my gut instincts?

My stress babies are always right. From now on, I will always listen to them.

Nothing feels like being hit by a car, like being hit by a car.

It was one thing in J...Jeremiah's book that I was always too scared to try. There are so many variables I couldn't plan out. But right then, the timing seemed right.

If I were flung off the side of the road and broke my neck, no harm no foul. I wanted to die anyway.

So, I waited, hidden in the trees until I saw headlights.

I fought all my instincts and jumped out into the middle of the road and braced for impact.

I thought I was dead.

My life flashed before my eyes.

Tires screeched. Thank God for anti-lock brakes. It's probably the only reason I'm not dead right now or in the hospital.

I smelled the burned tires as the car came to a stop inches from my shins.

The driver sat there, breathless, shaking, and shell-shocked.

She was sucking in air, in huge, gasping gulps for a good forty-five seconds before we both heard it: the sound of another car screeching around the turn. I immediately recognized the rattling of the engine.

It was Reckless Susie, my aunt.

By the time she finally saw us, it was too late. Susie slammed into the woman's rear bumper at a good clip. The momentum of the crash carried the car into my legs.

I flew backward into the brambles. I've got bruises on my legs the size of cantaloupes right now.

Not pretty.

“Oh my God!” Susie screamed as she jumped out of the car. Blood teemed from the other driver's nose onto the steering wheel. “Don't you know not to park in the middle of the road?! Well, don't you?!”

I watched the woman's shaky hand point in my direction. Susie's eyes drifted down the length of the woman's arm and tracked across the brambles, until they were finally level with my eyes. She caught me for an instant.

I ran. I couldn't be sure, but I swear I saw a glint of recognition on Susie's face before I disappeared.

BLUBBERING

Posted by Alex Dewitt × March 9 at 9:14 pm.

Delilah showed up at my door tonight, blubbering and blathering about Jeremiah letting her down and killing her dad.

She was wasted.

I don't even care anymore.

Honestly, she can have Jeremiah. He can have her drunken ass.

She can't expect me to drop everything to help her; she never did that for me.

It's a tough lesson, but if you can't help yourself, nobody will—even your best friend.

She'll feel better once she sleeps it off.

Somewhere else, though.

I'm done with her.

Seriously.

ACHES

Posted by Delilah Clark × March 10 at 4:51 pm.

My knees, shins, feet – basically the whole of both my legs – throbbed and ached the whole day. Every time I've stood, they shake and buckle. Just putting on pants was a struggle, but I gritted my teeth and bore it.

By the time I got home from school, my teeth were ground down into little nubs from holding in the pain.

All I wanted to do was lie in bed and whimper myself to sleep.

I should have just stayed home today. Maybe tomorrow.

ARRESTED

Posted by Delilah Clark × March 11 at 11:49 pm.

Soooo... I got arrested.

Not for truancy. Not for Frank's murder.

I got arrested for being hit by a car.

Terrence met me during lunch today and slapped the cuffs on me. I felt like a badass. I don't think anybody's been arrested at school in a long time. At least not since that pedo teacher got carted away a few years ago.

I thought he was bluffing, but he wasn't playing around. He spun me on my heels and lowered me into his car, a nasty, yellow Hyundai.

He was a little bit scary, actually. I didn't know Terry could be scary.

He sat me in the hot box. He deprived me of water. He turned the heat up to 11. It was all the classic police shtick you see in movies.

Finally, after what felt like hours of waiting, Terry walked in. His hands pressed against the shiny, metal table between us and he showed me two pictures; the first was Susie's rust bucket. The second was the car that hit me; a completely nondescript car with no remarkable features nor distinguishing marks. I wept for its owner's boring life.

"Two witnesses saw you flee the scene of an accident."

"A black-haired girl dressed all in black? And how did they get a good look at this alleged person in the pitch black?"

"One of the victims identified you by name."

It had to be Susie. Unless somehow a rando woman knew my name.

I asked for a lawyer, but one never appeared. I know better than to talk without a lawyer. Anybody that doesn't at this point, with YouTube, and TV, and movies all showing exactly why you need a lawyer, is an idiot.

He kept firing hearsay at me anyway. His case was circumstantial at best. A judge would never grant him a warrant.

I mean, what did he expect? A confession? I'd be a real idiot for admitting I was there, wouldn't I? I've seen enough cop shows to know that.

WHAT!

Posted by Alex Dewitt × March 12 at 3:01 pm.

So now I feel like a complete jerk.

Delilah came looking for help, I denied her, and she went and got herself arrested. Are you kidding me, Delilah?

I took one night off from worrying about your selfishness and you get arrested. What sixteen-year-old gets arrested when somebody hits **_them_** with a car?

Delilah. That's who. Queen of Drama. I swear to God it follows her around.

Delilah didn't even look phased when I went to see her. She blamed Susie for hitting her.

Let me say that again.

She jumped out in front of a car, which slammed on its brakes and was rear-ended by another car, and she blamed the DRIVER.

SHE JUMPED OUT IN FRONT OF THAT CAR HERSELF. On a dark highway.

Like people should know better.

"Susie should've killed me," she said. Only thing she said.

Not "Thanks for coming to get me in the middle of the night." or "Damn, that was stupid." or even "Hello."

No, just the same mopey-ass sentiment that she wished she was dead. Ungrateful. After all we do for her.

I could strangle her, but then she'd get what she wants.

DREAMS

Posted by Delilah Clark × March 13 at 6:07 am.

I had a ridiculous dream last night.

I was ten, being pushed on the swing by my dad. With every push, went a little higher, my little legs kicking at the heavens.

"Higher! Higher!" I said.

"I'm pushing. I'm pushing," Dad said. "I can only push so hard!"

The higher I went, the more ethereal he became, until I reached the apex of the swing and he burst into a white light.

Then, I jumped off.

I hung in the air, enjoying the pink sunset and the view from the heavens. I was in complete control—for about three seconds. Then my stomach dropped, and I fell like a rock straight down, crashing into the earth. I hit with a thud, bouncing on the concrete several times.

My father ran toward me. I could barely make out his mouth through the blinding white glow.

"I love you, Daddy," I said.

"I love you, too, pumpkin."

Suddenly, the soothing, white light faded away, replaced by a menacing, red one. A gunshot rang out.

Dad looked down; he was bleeding profusely from a gaping hole in his chest. As he dropped to his knees, I looked through the hole and saw Jeremiah cackling.

"You belong to me now," he said.

"No!" I screamed. "No. NO! DADDY!"

I woke up crying. I've never done that before. It was freaky.

NIGHT TERRORS

Posted by Delilah Clark × March 20 at 10:49 pm.

I keep having bad dreams about my dad and Jeremiah.

I'll wake up in shock two to three times a night and then have trouble falling back asleep.

I end up tossing and turning until the sun comes up.

It's gotten so bad; I've started sleeping on the floor in my dad's study again. It gives me a wicked crick in my neck and somehow our house has literally zero aspirin for some reason, but at least I can sleep soundly there.

I still don't know what it is. Laying in there feels like I'm wrapped in dad's arms. It feels safe.

LOCKBOX

Posted by Delilah Clark × March 23 at 1:19 am.

I found new evidence tonight!

Real, big boy evidence too! Not that tooth thing I've been touting this whole year.

Not stalking a complete nut job, like I've been doing with Jeremiah.

Real tangible motive.

Dad's study was unbearably cold tonight. I went looking for a second blanket. That's where I found it. In his closet, buried under mounds of crap, was a lockbox.

I'd ransacked the rest of the house looking for money, but I'd kept Dad's study relatively pristine; a monument to his life.

It was sealed with a combination lock. I couldn't pick it. Luckily, there's always another way. I took the lockbox outside and slammed the hinges against our oak tree.

The combination remained intact, but the hinges broke apart easily, and the lockbox swung open, revealing its secrets.

And holy crap were there secrets!

Inside was a treasure trove of information. There were Cayman bank account statements, ledgers of illegal activity, wire transfers, and documents from my Dad's company, GroupThink.

It was a mother lode of information. I don't know exactly what it means, but just by skimming through some of the financials, I could tell something nefarious was going on at GroupThink.

My dad was on to something big.

Big enough to kill for.

CAYMANS

Posted by Delilah Clark × March 25 at 9:24 am.

I don't think my dad was onto something nefarious. I think he was caught up in something nefarious.

There are all sorts of transfers from his company's account into ones all over the world.

They look like they dead end in the Caymans.

It looks like hundreds of thousands were funneled in there in the last ten years.

Is it possible my dad was super shady?

It's definitely food for thought, and it adds a lot of layers to why somebody would want him dead.

Whether he was into something shady, or was on to something shady, there's definitely motive for murder in these documents.

EVIDENCE

Posted by Delilah Clark × March 27 at 12:12 pm.

I've spent the last few days pouring over all the information from the lockbox, trying to figure out how it's all pieced together.

I've learned two things:

- There's a distinct possibility my dad was a jack-hole.
- There is something fishy going on at GroupThink.

I looked through my dad's notebook and cross referenced his boring numbers with those on the financials from GroupThink, and they synced up. Dates, times, numbers.

His computer had doctored bank statements and financials for every month that was in his lockbox.

It looks like he'd even been giving bogus financials to cover up his tracks. There was never much missing. In an account with millions changing hands every day, he would only pull out a few thousand every month.

I had every month's bank statements dating back ten years, except for the month he died.

September.

I needed that month.

Something happened in that month. I know it did.

FINANCIALS

Posted by Delilah Clark × March 29 at 8:33 pm.

This evidence is too much for me to bear. I'm not a financial analyst. I don't know if my dad is guilty of anything or a hero.

I don't care. This was enough evidence to prove he was murdered, or at least there was motive.

I need expert help. I need police help.

I need Terry's help.

LOSING MY MIND

Posted by Alex Dewitt × March 30 at 6:45 pm.

Alright. So, Delilah's come to me with some half-cocked stories in the past, but today she actually made sense. I must be losing my mind.

She showed me all sorts of financials and print outs and talked about schemes and money laundering, possible extortion, and real tangible reasons to prove her dad might have been murdered.

It was well thought out and made sense. On top of it all, she had real evidence to back it up.

So, I helped her deliver it to the police. For sure I helped her deliver it. I had to.

That detective, Terrence I think it was, only knew Delilah as a crazy person, but he'd always seen me as the voice of reason.

So, when I spoke up and told him that he needed to look at the evidence, I think it really meant something.

I think he'll look through it, or at least give it to somebody.

DELIVERY

Posted by Delilah Clark × March 30 at 8:53 pm.

I thought I would have to convince Alex to come with me. I thought I would have to pull her arm and agree to carry her first child to term.

But when I laid out the evidence, she actually believed we needed to go to the police. I couldn't believe it. I guess it helps to have something besides a tooth.

I'm glad, because Terry has always thought I was a wacko, but he never thought that of Alex.

He always thought she was just a good friend to me, trying to make the best out of a bad situation.

Terry might have dismissed me by myself, but when Alex stepped up and stood firm as she told him it was his duty to look at the evidence, he took notice.

She'd never believed me before.

I loved it. I wanted to kiss her right then and there. That's why she's my best friend, because she always sticks up for me.

Terry actually opened the box. He dug through the documents and his eyes went wide in astonishment. He asked where we got such a treasure trove of info.

I didn't have the heart to tell him that all I did was some detective work.

It was the first time I felt good about my life.

FINAL NOTICE

Posted by Delilah Clark × April 1 at 8:19 pm.

So, it finally came. I was waiting for it. The FINAL NOTICE letter from the bank.

It's just like all the others, but more menacing-y.

> *Dear Mr. and Mrs. Clark,*
>
> *Thank you very much for your patronage over the years. You have been loyal and valued customers. However, you have an outstanding balance in the amount of $27,532 that has been unresolved despite several calls and letters asking you to remit payment.*
>
> *If this is not paid by May 15, you will be forced to vacate the property and we will file the proper paperwork to have you relinquish any claim on the premises.*
>
> *Thank you and have a wonderful day,*
>
> *Joan Frederick*
>
> *Loan Officer*

We couldn't pay it. We didn't have $20 to our name, let alone $20,000.

I've been trying to tell them for months to give us more time. I've spilled our heartbreaking story dozens of times. I talked about a mother on disability, a father dead, a daughter working to support her family.

They didn't buy it. She offered to give me an extension for a couple days, but that was it.

I don't blame her. It's just her job. It's just business.

But I still hate her.

CRAZY SAUCE

Posted by Alex Dewitt × April 2 at 5:15 pm.

For the first time since her dad died, I thought Delilah might be on the right track. She found real, tangible evidence, and handed it over to the proper authorities.

It was a rational, sane decision. I actually had hope for her.

That lasted about a day.

Then, she went crazy sauce, talking about GroupThink and needing September financials. Saying that it was all in the September financials.

Now she's sure that her dad's boss killed him for some reason.

I want her to find the "killer". I want her to be happy. I want her to get help. I know they're about to lose the house, but she's just pressing now, grabbing at straws.

She keeps saying she's cracked open the case; all she needs is one more piece.

There's always one more piece. First it was the tooth. Then it was the lockbox. Now she says that piece is at GroupThink.

What am I going to do?

I have to help.

I've come this far.

GROUPTHINK

Posted by Delilah Clark × April 2 at 7:10 pm.

I needed that September financial statement. I knew it would break my dad's case wide open.

I tried finding a way to access it online, but dad didn't keep the passwords anywhere. I needed a hard copy. If anybody kept that stuff, it would be Edward, Dad's boss.

Maybe Dad's killer.

GroupThink has a meeting every morning. They last exactly 20 minutes. Dad complained about it all the time. "Why do they need 20 minutes?" "Why can't I just go on with my day?" "Edward just drones on and on!"

It was our best chance to get in and search for evidence.

So, after blowing off school, yet again—we walked into the brightly lit, yet sterile, marble office building of GroupThink, where we were greeted by Doris, the kindly, old receptionist working the front desk.

I sobbed that I needed something from Dad's desk. Something that Janie, his deskmate kept for me.

She was putty in my hands. I was a master at manipulation and she was my pawn.

Seconds later, Alex and I walked through two, glass, double doors and into the main office area.

The modern office: sleek, metallic, devoid of all character, and filled with drones who waved goodbye to independent thought decades ago in exchange for some semblance of financial security. It's only once they get fired for picking their nose, or having an independent thought, that they realize what a waste of life they've been.

We hid in the corner until Edward strolled out of a small hallway and tapped vigorously on his watch.

"MEETING TIME!" he shouted. "Conference room in thirty seconds! Let's go, people. Let's goooo! Time is money and money is DEFINITELY money."

Everybody hopped up and ran toward the conference room, desperate not to be the last person seated.

We had exactly 20 minutes.

I watched as the last straggler ran inside and shut the door. Once everyone was in, we ran through the cubicles and around a corner—into the hallway Edward had just vacated. His office was toward the end of the long hallway, past the bathrooms, and behind a flimsy door.

I turned the knob on his office door, but it was locked. Clearly Edward was adept at keeping his secrets just that, secret.

Luckily, I always had a key. I pulled the bobby pins out of my hair and went to work. In no time, the pins bent to my will and we were inside.

I turned my attention to a large closet. Inside I found wall-to-wall boxes, all labeled in a similar manner: 012012, 022012, 032012, and so on. Every box was labeled clearly and in descending numerical order. Multiple boxes were being labeled like this: 022012(1), 022012(2), 022012(3) - but that's complicated and boring, and pretty much irrelevant to the story. It doesn't take a rocket scientist to figure out they were categorized by month and year.

I found the one box labeled 092014. It contained every correspondence and piece of information Edward deemed important from the month my dad died. If there a bank statement, that's where it would be.

We began digging, through a metric ton of information, packed to the hilt and unorganized to boot. It isn't normal for somebody like Edward to throw everything in a box haphazardly. It almost seemed like he dug through it in a rush, looking for something, and had been too flustered to place it back properly.

Alex dug down into the deepest, darkest depths of that box, until she hit the jackpot - a crumpled piece of paper with a Post-it Note on it.

I grabbed the statement and read it over. It was exactly what I was looking for, GroupThink's September bank statement, complete with a Post-it Note saying:

$750K Discrepancy. Too much??

I'd done the math and only found $250K transferred between the two accounts over the past ten years, so a $750K ramp up in one month would be something of a huge development.

It would certainly be noteworthy. It would certainly be kill-worthy.

I needed to get this into Terry's hands, after I'd looked it over for a couple of days first, of course.

THE OVEN

Posted by Delilah Clark × April 3 at 9:54 pm.

I did something really stupid tonight. I have to get this out quick because they're coming to take me back to the loony bin.

I really messed up.

I am trying to barricade myself in my room for a minute, but they are coming, and I won't be able to keep them away for long.

It's not even a big deal, but my mom and Susie are seriously overreacting.

Mom and Susie were gone when I got home today. There was a note on the counter to preheat the oven and start dinner.

I flipped the oven on and stared at the glass as it glowed a bright red. I couldn't help, but remember what J, I mean Jeremiah, wrote about sticking his head in the oven to kill himself.

> I know this was a normal practice several decades ago,
> but I don't understand it. My head just got really, really
> hot. I couldn't take it anymore, so I pulled it out
> and made some french fries. They kind
> of tasted like burned hair.

It made me chuckle, honestly. The stuff that kid couldn't get right, could just about fill the Grand Canyon.

It had been a while since I'd abandoned my suicide studies. It used to consume me, but with my father's case, my extracurricular pursuits were lost in the shuffle.

I peered into the encompassing blackness of my house, looking for anything or anyone that might be lurking. Confident I wasn't being watched, I scooted over, took the casserole out of the oven and stuck my head inside.

At that moment, the lights flickered on and the back door creaked open. Susie and Mom entered the kitchen, carrying groceries and shopping bags. They dropped their bags. A cantaloupe rolled up to my shoe. My mother screamed for a good thirty seconds. I jerked my head out of the oven and slammed the door.

"It's not what you think," I blurted out. But it was too late. Susie was already calling the doctors. I ran into my room.

Now, I'm screwed. Goodbye house, goodbye life. Goodbye all of it.

And that's about that, swim fans. I don't know when I'll be seeing you, but I'll be seeing you. Hope you've enjoyed it. Keep your fingers crossed they don't give me electroshock or "Cuckoo's Nest" me.

I shouldn't make jokes. In all fairness, I am legit scared.

Crap! That's them.

They're about to beat down the door. Alex, if you're reading this, come see me whenever you can!

I have the bank statement!

VISITING HOURS

Posted by Alex Dewitt × April 7 at 6:01 pm.

It took me four days to see Delilah. I guess they keep you on a 72-hour suicide watch when you go crazy.

I saved her blog. I set it on private. Nobody else will read it. I didn't even read it. Not until now. There's some messed up things on there. Like really messed up.

Also, I really don't like that she told you all I was nearly raped and then peed in the bushes. Even if it was private...that doesn't make it any less messed up.

When I finally did get to see her, all she did was babble about looking over her precious blog while she was at the asylum. I couldn't refuse. She looked so pathetic.

She wore a white jumpsuit and was quite sullen; much more than usual. Even at her most depressed, there was always a twinkle in her eye, but now that's gone. I think not knowing how long she'll be locked up inside is wearing on her.

"How is it?" I asked.

She lied. We both knew it. "Not bad. I'm on the fourth floor. There's a window, so I can look out on all the pretty, sane people."

"Did you really want to kill yourself?"

Delilah looked off into the distance. "Sometimes. Who doesn't?"

My eyes welled. I couldn't think of anything to say that would comfort my friend. It was horrible. The guard tapped his watch. It was time to go.

"I'll be back tomorrow," I said.

BENNETT – PRIVATE

Posted by Delilah Clark × April 9 at 4:11 pm.

Delilah is looking a little worse for wear these days. She's blubbering a bit, and her face is pastier than normal. She's been crying in her cell.

When I left today, she palmed a letter into my hand.

She whispered into my ear before they dragged her away. "Post this word for *word*".

So here it goes. These are her words, not mine.

____

I sat in an empty white room, save for two metal chairs. It was cold, not just in temperature but also in ambiance. I felt more like a criminal than a patient.

They've housed some of the criminally insane in this ward. I suspect this room must be where they take them for interrogations. The red light blinked on a security camera in the corner. I waved at the technician who must be watching me, bored out of his mind.

I still don't understand why I'm here, though. Up until this point my sessions were conducted by a lovely, female psychiatrist whose office smelled of lilacs. She was just out of medical school, so it was super easy to manipulate her.

When the heavy, metal door to the room creaked open, I smelled Bennett's aftershave and let out a groan. "I hate metal chairs."

He slid his clipboard underneath him. "Much better."

"Just don't fart," I said. "Wouldn't want those important papers to stink, would we?"

I stared up at the security camera in the corner of the room. The red light wasn't blinking anymore. "Don't worry," Bennett said. "I had it turned off. This is a safe place where we can openly share our feelings."

"I have nothing to say to you."

Bennett and I locked eyes in an epic stare down. I'd had epic ones with him in the past, but this took the cake by a country mile.

Minutes turned to hours, hours to days, days to weeks, until finally, I broke. I just couldn't take it anymore. Talking with crazies all day makes you yearn for any companionship...even if it's from a chode.

"Why are you here?" I asked.

Bennett shook his head. "I'm on special assignment for the hospital."

Special assignment? That didn't make sense to me. I'm just a little girl with daddy issues. I wasn't buying it. There had to be someone more worthy of his time.

"I have my reasons," he said. Then he told me to get used to it because I'd be having sessions with him from now on.

I wasn't ready. I will never be ready for that. The one thing I enjoyed about the asylum was not having to deal with him anymore.

Eventually he stood up.

"I think that's enough for today. However, know this, the sooner you talk this through, the sooner we can send you home."

I have no idea what just happened. But something smells fishy. I know this is a small town, but for Bennett and the hospital to take such an interest in one girl doesn't seem right. Keep an eye out, true believers.

That's the entire message from Delilah. I'm starting to get nervous that something bad might happen to her.

I agree with her that something isn't right. Why would Bennett take such an interest in her?

EXCHANGE

Posted by Alex Dewitt × April 10 at 11:23 am.

Delilah finally got me the GroupThink bank statement she's been hoarding in her jumpsuit for the past couple weeks.

The asylum has a strict not touching policy, so it was dicey to get the exchange going, but we finally just went for it.

What's the worst that happens to Delilah at this point, really? I mean they can't keep her more locked up.

DYNAMITE

Posted by Alex Dewitt × April 11 at 9:49 pm.

Just when you think nothing else could go wrong in life…BOOM goes the dynamite. No. It's not dynamite. It's an A-bomb. Maybe an H-bomb.

I delivered the bank statement to Terrence today. I thought he would flip his lid. I mean a $750k discrepancy in one month had to move some sort of needle. It had to prove something.

But he wasn't even phased. Because he knew.

He had been onto Tim for six months. They'd brought him in for questioning half a dozen times.

Never for a minute did Tim stop denying his innocence, but the police had enough on him for a life sentence or two. Embezzlement, tax fraud, larceny, and a litany of other charges.

They intended to indict when he dropped Edward's name. He was the big dog. The prospect of taking him down enticed Terrence and the rest of the force.

Tim promised to delivery Edward in return for immunity. He delivered mounds of evidence, but every clue turned up a dead end. A dead end that led back to Tim. Eventually, they just stopped listening.

They gave him one last chance. A chance to go in with a wire and force a confession out of Edward. The confessions would've cleared his name, but Tim killed himself the night before it was supposed to go down.

Terrence sighed as he finished. "Must've known he couldn't pull it off. It's hard to propagate a lie. Even harder when you get caught."

That was a load of bull. I didn't buy it, but he did. So did the whole department. He told me flat out that they put the case against Edward to bed the day they zipped up Tim's body bag.

I was livid. "Well if that's true, you guys are terrible detectives. Best case scenario, you drove a man to suicide. Worst case scenario, you're letting a murderer run free."

I stormed off. I couldn't look at Terrence anymore. I now know why Delilah has such disdain for him.

Even though she's crazy, I'm starting to believe she might've stumbled on to something real. Maybe Edward really did kill her dad.

People have killed for less than $750k.

OUT – PRIVATE

Posted by Delilah Clark × April 19 at 7:23 pm.

And I'm back.

It turns out they can't keep you in an asylum when you're not crazy. They can ask you questions though.

They can do some tests, but if you pass them all, they have to release you.

I guess I could have voluntarily stayed in there and kept talking to Bennett all day, every day, but I definitely did not want that.

He's the worst.

And he's obsessed with my dad.

Like for real for real obsessed.

Almost as obsessed as I am.

THE TRUTH – PRIVATE

Posted by Delilah Clark × April 21 at 9:10 am.

I'll bet you're wondering if the asylum was awful. Well it was! Here's a list of all the things that are awful about that place:

      1. Everything.
      2. See point 1.

Seriously, that place was the worst. Not only was the food inedible, but the rooms were freezing, the beds had no sheets, and the company was atrocious. Not the inmates—they were fine—but the guards and staff are wastes of life! I've never met people so boring in my life. I mean their jobs are literally subduing crazy people, so you would think they had oodles of interesting stories. NOPE!

Second, Bennett had me on lockdown.

Nobody could see me. Nobody could talk to me. People didn't even acknowledge my existence. Even the staff had trouble tracking me down at times.

Third, check this out. Bennett is a tool.

He knew my father!

He treated my father for YEARS before my dad died. Did you know my dad saw a shrink? I didn't.

Don't you think that's something a psychologist should tell their patient, that maybe there's a conflict of interest there?

What a freak!

WEIRDO – PRIVATE

Posted by Delilah Clark × April 22 at 3:47 pm.

There were a lot of weirdos in the asylum. There were a lot of normals having nervous breakdowns, or on 72-hour suicide watch – ah, memories – but there were a lot of weirdos.

By far and away the biggest weirdo of all was Bennett.

He was weirder than the guy wearing makeup and pretending he was Phyllis Diller.

He was weirder than the woman barking on all fours like a dog all day. He was weirder than the couple who swore they were Siamese twins.

It was like he wanted me all to himself.

After I palmed that bank statement to Alex, he convinced my mom to keep me on lockdown "for my own good." We would have marathon sessions where he drilled me with questions about my dad, about my life, about my investigation.

I obfuscated the best I could, but the longer I was inside the more I opened up. I couldn't help it. He asked me the same question in thirty different ways until my mind was jumbled and scrambled.

Eventually, I told him everything.

I told him about Edward. I told him about the bank statements. I told him about the sneaky stuff my dad was into, and he just listened. With every word out of my mouth he locked me down tighter.

He seemed almost to admire my dad. He kept saying that my dad's only crime was caring too much about money, which is the human condition.

"I care about money, too," he said. "It takes a lot to run a business and keep up appearances."

That's weird, right?

CONTRITE – PRIVATE

Posted by Delilah Clark × April 24 at 8:11 pm.

Terry came to my house today. His head slung low and kicking rocks.

"Edward is dead," he told me.

All our evidence convinced him to do some real police work, so he decided to investigate Edward on his off days.

After a few days tailing him, Edward stopped showing up for work. Then he stopped leaving his house. Terry thought he might've skipped town.

That's when he got a warrant.

"I knocked, but there was no answer. There were no signs of life, only a smell. A putrid smell. The smell of death. I broke one of the panes out of the door, reached in, unlocked it, and entered. I didn't get two steps inside before I saw a foot lying in the hallway. I called out to Edward, but there was no answer. When I entered the living room, I saw Edward's body. Rigid. Sitting on a desk chair."

He was dead. There was no sign of forced entry. There was no sign of a struggle.

The third such death since the school year started. We haven't had a death in East Willow in a long time. Now there have been three.

It was too much to just be a coincidence. First my father, then the grave broker, now Edward. All of them dead with no sign of forced entry. I didn't know how they were all connected, but there had to be a connection.

PROPS

Posted by Alex Dewitt × April 25 at 9:15 am.

The dance is tomorrow. I have nothing done. Literally, nothing done. I've stayed up all night, every night this week. I didn't update this blog. I didn't take Delilah's calls. I didn't do anything. Except work.

And even with all my work, I only got half of what I needed to do done. I was ready to call it all off, maybe bomb the gym, or call in an air strike. I thought it was going to be a disaster.

That is until I walked into the gym today and saw it completely decorated. Moses was putting the finishing touches on the balloon drop. Another person was hanging stars on the ceilings, and a third was testing the sound for the DJ booth.

They did it all. And it was perfect. Moses is kind of amazing.

I was in such a shame spiral that I didn't have time to pull anything together for this stupid dance, but Moses came through.

He sold more tickets in a week than I did in months. They were sold mostly to the freaks and geeks, but they're people, too. I can't wait to see everybody freak out when their dance is full of nerds. Ah sweet, sweet revenge.

Conventional wisdom says the popular people should plan dances since they're hip and cool, but that's not true. It was way better than I could have done. I focused on the wrong people. I focused on the bad people. Not the good ones.

And Moses is a good one.

PIECES – PRIVATE
Posted by Delilah Clark × May 25 at 4:11 pm.

Dad would appreciate this puzzle. It's a real doozie.

What do Edward, Frank, and my father have in common?

Two of the three are easy. But what about the third? What does Frank have to do with any of this?

Does he have something to do with it, or was he just an unfortunate and coincidental byproduct?

That would be easy, but TV taught me there is no such thing as a coincidence.

BINGO – PRIVATE

Posted by Delilah Clark × April 25 at 4:11 pm.

I got it.

I know what happened.

All it took was tracking down Frank's business name, cross-referencing it with the path GroupThink's money went through to—

Know what. I'm not going to say. I don't want to tip anybody off.

I have to find Alex. We have to end this tonight, before the killer strikes again.

DANCEY PANTSY – PRIVATE

Posted by Delilah Clark × April 27 at 1:11 am.

I couldn't find Alex all day. I guess that's what happens when you're running a dance committee all by yourself.

Or surprisingly with the help of Moses, somehow. I'll have to ask about that later.

So, I was forced to go to the dance. I mean I might've gone anyway, but at least I had the choice before.

A small part of me wanted to be girly and dress up. Let me note, though, it was a very small part. The majority of me wanted to wear sweatpants and eat cookie dough. But I bought a black dress and gussied myself up all the same.

There were streamers and stars, clovers, and rainbows. It was like a Lucky Charms box exploded in our gym. Very classy. I liked it

What I didn't like were the people. When I finally got to the school, the gym was packed to the gills.

Half the student body was crowded inside, bumping and grinding. The other half formed a line that snaked around the building.

Alex stood in the middle of it all getting all the kudos she deserved. It really was incredible she pulled it off. I don't know who she had to blow to get it done, but it came out dope. The old me would have squealed in delight.

So, there was dancing and revelry and generally smiles all around. Not from me, but from everybody else.

It was impossible to pin Alex down. She was bouncing back and forth like a rubber ball all night. So, I was stuck hanging by myself all night, except that time I danced with Moses.

Yes, I danced with Moses. I figured I owed him for helping me with Alex all those months ago and again for helping her make the dance slamming. Seriously, I had no idea nerds had such mad DJ skills.

Moses pulled me out onto the dance floor as the music turned from a high-octane, pulse-pounding, indistinguishable dance song to a slow one that only has one purpose: to let guys sniff their date's hair and allow girls to be held by the small of their backs.

Moses moved to grab me around the waist, but I quickly jumped back, embarrassed. We ended up dancing like 7th graders, with a chasm of space between us and our hands barely touching each other's shoulders.

Honestly though, I didn't hate it. There was something about Moses that felt comfortable. I trusted him. I didn't trust many people.

"Ever just get the need to destroy something beautiful, Moses?"

I found his lips curling upward in a half smile. "No."

I found myself enjoying Moses in that moment, which was unacceptable. I couldn't have that. I couldn't allow myself to enjoy anything, so I pushed him away and sulked for the rest of the dance.

Eventually, the clock struck midnight, the last of my classmates funneled into the parking lot, and Alex the party planner, turned back into the pumpkin that was Alex, my friend.

That's when I told her everything, which I can't tell you, just in case that stalker nutcase is reading this.

WOW

Posted by Alex Dewitt × April 28th at 3:14 am.

That escalated quickly. I'll never understand why I do the things I do for Delilah. Why does she insist on ruining my good time?

All I wanted to do this weekend was bask in the glow of my unintended success. Then go home, soak my feet, and reminisce about how amazing the dance turned out. Was that too much to ask? Apparently so.

I'm very happy that she decided to come at all, but why did she have to give me a sneaky Pete mission to accomplish? And why would she need me to do it ASAP? Couldn't she just say good job?

I guess with my now criminal history of breaking into places, Delilah thought having me break into Bennett's office and steal confidential patient files would go over great.

Well it didn't. I didn't like it one bit.

Did I still go through with it though?

Yes.

And Delilah was totally right. Her psychologist is a world-class scumbag. He had files on everybody in town, blackmailing them and extorting sex from them in exchange for his silence.

His biggest files were on Tim, Edward, and this other guy named Frank that Delilah said was a grave broker. I don't know what that means, or why somebody would do that.

What a show, man.

MISSION – PRIVATE

Posted by Delilah Clark × April 29 at 3:01 am.

It was a dangerous mission, but Alex pulled it off.

She had to sneak into Bennett's office and steal a bunch of patient files. If I was right, he would have fat files on Edward, Frank, and my dad.

Lo and behold – he did. Pages upon pages of them. Whole reams of paper.

I have to go through them one by one and scan them before I give them to the police, just in case they screw it up and miss something.

P.S. Rest assured, even though Alex's mission was dangerous, mine was worse. I had to have dinner with Bennett while she was ransacking his place. I had to talk about my feelings.

And I had to not kill him. That was the hardest part.

COMBING – PRIVATE

Posted by Delilah Clark × May 1 at 1:21 pm.

Now that the evidence is in police custody, and arrest is imminent, I can reveal what I pieced together.

God, I hope the police are at least as intelligent as a group, as I am by myself.

1. Dad and Edward have been scamming GroupThink for years, maybe for as long as I've been alive.
2. Dad was the finance guy, and Edward smoothed everything over with the board.
3. With over 10,000 transactions a month flying through that place, nobody noticed a few hundred dollars here and a couple thousand there go missing. I mean the Feds lose hundreds of billions in unaccounted for money every year and nobody bats an eye.
4. Over the long haul, they had quite a nest egg, over $250,000 and counting, gathering interest. Figure another 10-20 years of working they'd walk away with millions easy.

But where did Frank come in?

They needed somewhere to wash the money when it came out of GroupThink. They couldn't just make it go offshore right away. That would be too suspicious.

So, they created a contractor in their books. I saw him over and over again. Gravel Rob. I thought it was weird to hire a paving company every year for months at a time but didn't think anything of it.

Then it clicked. Grave Rob.

Dad and Edward funneled their money to Frank. Frank did whatever laundering was, and it came back clean.

The files Alex recovered showed the connection between them all: Edward and Frank were high school buddies that lost touch over the years.

Pretty much untraceable.

Until Bennett came along.

What does Bennett have to do with it?

Years of underhanded dealings weighed on my dad. He fought with it himself for years, but it became too much for him. He couldn't tell my mom, or me, or anybody.

So, he found a psychologist. He found the *wrong* psychologist.

Bennett kept files on every one of his patients, blackmailing them for sex, or money, or just for a laugh.

And my dad was a whale.

About a year ago, money started siphoning out of Dad's accounts into cash check transfers.

After cross checking all of those transfers against Bennett's notes, I found a pattern.

Each transfer corresponded with a check, which corresponded with a session my dad had with Bennett. He labeled each session that he extorted money from my dad with a "$" at the end of the date. In the margins he wrote how much Dad gave him.

Eventually, Bennett got greedy. He started asking for more and more and more, until he demanded the whole kit and caboodle. $750,000 dollars, or he'd go to the police.

And Dad did it. Dad got him the money.

Then Dad died, yet Bennett *still* wasn't satisfied. I don't know why Bennett killed Dad. Maybe Dad gave him an ultimatum that this was the last straw. Maybe

Bennett didn't like that. All I know is that Bennett killed my dad after that transaction. But he still wasn't satisfied.

He went to Edward, who continued to funnel him money for a while, until about March then it all stopped.

Suddenly Frank died.

The transfers didn't start again.

Then Edward died.

All of the notes plus the financials pointed to one thing.

Bennett blackmailed, then killed my dad after he got the huge transfer completed. Then he went after Edward and Frank.

Then he killed Frank.

Then Edward.

That wraps it all up in a nice bow, huh?

SCUMBAG

Posted by Delilah Clark × May 5 at 11:47 pm.

They arrested Bennett today. I worried they weren't going to do it.   worried that he was going to walk free, or that he was going to read my diary and flee the country.

Then I remembered, I never took it off private. Duh!

But now he's behind bars, and he'll stay that way for a long time.

I always had a hunch he was weird, but there were a couple of things that gave him away:

1. When I met Edward at Bennett's office, they shared a look that was completely different than the thousands of scared baby goat looks I've seen from people coming out of Bennett's office before or since.
2. That conversation he had with me at the asylum wherein he told me he knew my dad.
3. More than that, he kept me guarded, locked away in that asylum so that nobody could find me. It was like he didn't want me to talk to anybody. Like I was on to something; getting too close. I mean that tooth ended up being bonkers, but I let slip about the lockbox I found in Dad's study and my meeting with Edward, and clearly, he didn't like that.
4. People kept dying, right after I talked to Bennett about them, with the exception of my dad. I brought up the grave broker to him in session; two days later he was dead. I brought up Edward and GroupThink; a week later he was dead.

Or maybe it was a big coincidence, and I just happened to stumble onto things. I was in the right place at the right time and I caught the wrong guy doing the wrong thing. I don't know, but I feel good – like a giant weight has been lifted off my chest. My dad's killer is finally behind bars.

CATHARSIS

Posted by Delilah Clark x May 6 at 11:27 pm.

I came home today to find Moses on my front porch, baseball bats lying on both sides of him.

"You wanted to destroy something beautiful. I want to help."

He didn't get it. I wasn't talking about actually destroying something beautiful. I was all pent up about Bennett and grossed out by how I wasn't grossed out by Moses's touch.

"I'm not going to beat your skull in," I replied. "No matter how appealing that might be. Also, kind of ballsy to think you're beautiful."

Moses shook his head. "No. I was thinking, I don't know, maybe we smash some mailboxes, or the bird feeder at the park."

I picked up one of the baseball bats and swung it a few times. Suddenly, I really did want to destroy something.

Something beautiful.

Or at least something Dad thought was beautiful.

Something my dad loved. I totally get my Mom's vehemence toward him now. Unlike her though, I wanted my catharsis.

It took a while for me to figure out how to lurch my dad's car forward, but eventually I popped the clutch and ground the gears enough times to make it to an empty field near our house.

I tossed Moses a bat while I took one of my own. I remember my father teaching me how to swing a bat. He told me to spit on the ground before stepping up to the plate, waggle the bat in your hands, and pivot your hips to maximize bat speed.

And I did. I swung as hard as I could and connected clean with the right side-view mirror. The glass splintered, and the mirror flew halfway across the field.

It felt amazing—a year's worth of pent-up frustration surging out of me.

I cried.

Tears of joy, frustration, and sadness flew out of me. It was the first time I'd been emotional about anything in a long time.

I spent the next hour or two destroying my father's car. I had cracked all the windows. I punctured all the tires with a broken bit of glass. I tore up the seats and ripped out the glove box. Sometimes Moses took a crack himself, but mostly he just watched.

When I was finally finished, my chest heaved uncontrollably.

I turned to Moses and laughed a nervous laugh born not of happiness, but of catharsis. I collapsed into Moses's arms. We didn't say anything.

He just held me.

For the first time in a long time, I felt safe.

TELLING MOM

Posted by Delilah Clark × May 8 at 11:11 am.

My mom is one weird cat, man. I don't understand her one bit.

Get this.

I figured, that with everything that had happened and everything I'd put her through, that she deserved an explanation. I owed it to her.

You know, so she wouldn't be so freaked out about us losing the house, so she could stop packing.

I thought she would be soo happy.

Instead, she totally grounded me!

I found her packing up our stuff. The last remnants of our life. We only have a week to get together the money before the bank takes everything. We still have no backup plan. Only she didn't know we didn't need one.

"You can stop doing this now," I said.

Then I told her the whole story. I won't bore you, but I covered every disgusting, horrifying, and amazing detail you've read in the past year.

At the end of the story, my mom sat, stunned. I expected her to wrap her arms around me and thank me.

I expected tears of joy or a "praise Jesus," or something. But she sat in silence. Then, she let out a tirade like I've never heard, cursing, screaming and flailing her arms.

"I can't believe—behind my back—total lack of respect—" was what I could pick out. But then she grounded me! Like forever!

She's got to be crazy if she thinks that's going to stick, but still!

I don't know what her problem is.

LEGEND

Posted by Delilah Clark × May 9 at 11:11 am.

I'm a bit of a legend. I'm already passing into myth.

Front page of this morning's paper, above the fold. Four columns.

LOCAL GIRL SOLVES MYSTERY; AVENGES FATHER'S DEATH

I'm so going to frame every juicy word. Here's one of my favorite passages:

> *After a year of meticulously gathering evidence, Delilah Clark finally has solace.*

I did feel solace. More so, I felt vindication. Alex even got her props:

> *The arrest would not have been possible without Alex Dewitt's heroism and bravery. She was the one that found the crucial piece of evidence hidden among the alleged perpetrator's files and bravely delivered them to the authorities.*

I'm getting 100 copies and sending notes with them that say, "EAT A DICK" to everybody who doubted me.

That is sweet justice.

ACCEPTANCE

Posted by Delilah Clark × May 10 at 12:31 pm.

I was sitting in my room today when a thought occurred to me. A thought I'd put out of my brain when there was more to do. It exploded in my brain like a firecracker.

Holy crap, did I ever get into that Harvard program?

Luckily, I haven't cleaned my room, not even once, since my dad's death.

There were papers on top of papers, on top of papers, scattered around the room, and frankly I didn't remember where I threw it. I rummaged around the dankest darkest corners of my room and sure enough, it was still there, where I threw it all those months ago.

I didn't read it all, but I got the gist.

> *Congratulations—*
> *—Summer term—*
> *Look forward—having you enrolled.*

That's all I needed. I got in! For the first time in a long time, I was thrilled.

PRAISE

Posted by Alex Dewitt × May 10 at 6:13 pm.

People have been coming up to me all week. They can't believe I planned this whole dance, all by my little lonesome, while helping Delilah catch a killer.

People are sheep.

Of course, I didn't plan it at all, did I? Nor did I do much to help catch anybody. I mean I was there, sure, and I broke into a couple places, but I wasn't very supportive.

I really just tore Delilah down all year. I mean she totally deserved it. She was nuts.

But she was also right. I can't believe she ended up being right.

Not about abandoning me. She definitely wasn't right about that.

I still hate her a little for that.

OLD TIMES

Posted by Alex Dewitt × May 11 at 6:13 pm.

The old Delilah is peeking through again.

She even wore a pink shirt to school yesterday. Her "Alex is #1" sh rt. I love that shirt.

We actually went out to dinner and sat together.

She even laughed...once.

She told me she was going to Harvard. Can you believe it? Harvard?

Early admission to their summer program? Harvard. After the year she had?

Unbelievable.

I hope she can make up all that work.

They'll never let her in if they see her grades this semester.

THE NEW PSYCHOLOGIST

Posted by Delilah Clark × May 12 at 6:41 pm.

As part of the agreement to keep me out a straitjacket, the asylum put me in touch with a new psychologist.

Not one who knew my father or was plotting some horrendous coup of my body or mind—this one is actually all right.

Maybe it's because I've matured, or maybe it's because the guy isn't a sociopath.

His name is Harris Allen. He is clean-shaven and baby-faced. I doubt he's more than five years out of school. And he has a strange habit of cocking his head from one side to the other as he listens to my stories.

Generally, I like our conversations. It's good to talk with somebody who doesn't know me in the slightest. Of course, every word out of my mouth makes me realize what a ridiculous experience I went through this past year. And he was very honest with me.

"What's the damage, Doc?" I said after one session. "You think I'm crazy too, huh?"

He laughed. "I think that you're obviously very upset about your father's death—and with intensive help, I think you'll learn to cope."

I smiled and leaned back. I liked the thought of that.

SUSIE

Posted by Delilah Clark × May 13 at 11:41 pm.

After dinner tonight, I went out with Susie.

I haven't spoken to her much since the car accident. She's still been driving me to my psychology appointments, but she hasn't been pleasant about it.

It had been about her sense of obligation to the family, not from any deeper sense of affection for me, and it was making me uncomfortable.

We'd always been kind of close, in our weird way, and I wasn't happy with the way things were going.

Today I'd had enough of it.

"Thanks," I said to her.

It was the first word besides "Hi" I'd said to her in weeks. "For—you know. And Sue…I'm sorry."

She nodded to me. That's all we needed. She isn't one to mince words, and neither am I.

Don't know if our relationship will ever get to where it was before, but it's a start.

DINNER

Posted by Alex Dewitt × May 14 at 8:14 am.

It feels normal again, almost.

With this year of Hell winding down, I finally sat down with Delilah and Kendra.

Kendra has come out of her stupor a bit. She even strung three sentences together while I was there.

It's a building process, but it's something. The weight of foreclosure is almost off her head.

Tim's life insurance check has been approved. Delilah's going to pick it up in two days.

Amazing what the unburdening of finances can do to a person.

Kendra walks lighter now. She had been developing a hunch in her back that grew deeper with each passing month.

Now, she stands up straight. She even started taking some college certification courses to qualify for a job.

She's going to be all right.

I think we all are.

CHILLS

Posted by Delilah Clark × May 15 at 9:21 pm.

I saw Bennett today.

He was cold, calloused. He had no remorse for what he'd done. I asked him why, why would he kill my dad, Edward, and the grave broker.

He smirked. "Things are not always so easy for grown-ups. One of the great things about youth is that money is never a factor. You never really think about it, unless you need some bubble gum, or a new car, or God forbid, an abortion."

Bennett swallowed. "But for people like your father and me, we worried about money all the time. All. The. Time."

"So, is that it then? It was just money? I was kind of hoping there was some greater plan of evil."

"Sorry to disappoint. Enough money can make a man do anything. Look at me. I used to be an upstanding citizen."

It may be the worst story I've ever heard.

It's definitely up there.

He was a sociopath with no remorse, as if killing my dad were as mundane as eating a turkey sandwich. I wanted to slit his throat right then and there. I wanted him to hurt like I hurt.

Hopefully, spending the next three lifetimes behind bars will give him a chance to repent.

ANTOINE

Posted by Delilah Clark × May 16 at 10:18 pm.

Finally got to see that jag-weed life insurance adjuster again today.

Could he be any more last minute? He canceled on me four times. I mean it's a lot of money to scrounge up, but I really needed that phat nut.

Well, it would have been a lot of money, if dad didn't mess it all up. I can't believe how much he screwed things up for us, even from beyond the grave.

I was all smiles biking down to the life insurance agency. I couldn't wait to be the hero.

A quarter of a million dollars makes up for quite a lot of bad times. But when Antoine handed me the check, my face dropped. It was only for $75,000.

It had to be wrong. I was SURE my dad had a quarter-million-dollar policy.

Turned out, my dad had taken out a heavy lien against the policy. Multiple heavy liens.

We were actually quite lucky it paid out or we could've been looking at a hefty bill.

$75,000 was all that remained.

My happiness turned to dread.

Sure, we could pay off the housing lien, but what then?

I can't go to Harvard or do anything we need to do in order to keep my mother from falling apart.

It's an awful feeling, failing miserably.

At least I can take some solace in paying off our foreclosure debt.

It buys us some time, but we'll just be here again in a few months, or years. It's not enough to set my mom up for her future.

TAKETH

Posted by Alex Dewitt × May 17 at 3:14 pm.

Damn.

The Lord giveth and the Lord taketh away, huh?

Just a couple days ago, Delilah was set for life. The life insurance was gonna pay off the house, Harvard, and give Kendra room to live comfortably for the rest of her days.

It's amazing what a couple days can do.

Men are jerks. Turns out Tim took out gobs of cash to finance his ridiculous life style.

I guess he figured it wouldn't matter, since he had decades of work to repay it.

Unfortunately, that wasn't the case.

 Now, Delilah and Kendra barely have enough to get even with the house. Delilah is crestfallen. She can't even talk. Harvard is out of the question.

College is out of the question almost, unless she wants crippling debt, or she gets a miraculous scholarship.

Delilah always wanted to do better than the townies that go to community college. I'll get out. My parents are loaded and connected. I can go anywhere, but Delilah... she's stuck here.

Stuck in East Willow forever. A fate worse than death.

THE CODE

Posted by Delilah Clark × May 18 at 7:43 pm.

I'd just gotten home from the bank. I'd given the foreclosure people nearly every dollar of my father's policy in order to pacify them for a while, and I was pissed.

I walked up the stairs and looked at my dad's study.

My heart was in my throat. I'd thought I could help, but it turned out like everything else in my life—fruitless.

I bought my trusty baseball bat into dad's office. The stain on the floor was now an appropriate homage to my father's life.

A guttural wail born out of pain, agony, and infinite sadness, rose up from within me. My anger overpowered me, and I began to smash everything in his office; nothing was safe.

I dented the file cabinet, I smashed the windows, and knocked stacks of papers on the floor. I broke the desk in two and threw the computer to the floor.

It booted up, even across the room, and loaded the homepage – the Bank of the Grand Caymans right before my dad fumbled to turn the monitor off.

I threw down the bat and knelt down on the floor. The page loaded and asked for an account number.

I had no idea what it could possibly be. Since my dad was a secretive dude, I doubt he just put them on one of the sloppily organized Post-it notes, though that would be a really cool puzzle. Then, it hit me. *My dad loved puzzles.*

At the bottom of the screen was a "Forgot Account Number?" button. I clicked on it and a question popped up.

Security Question: Half of 12 would I be, as with if you doubled 3.

The number six was the answer, but that didn't help me at all. I mean there's no way the bank account number was six. Maybe in the 60s, but not today with the sophisticated passwords they force you to input.

Then I remembered the riddles my dad would always tell me. He said them exactly the same every time. *And there were six of them!*

> A man was born in 1955. He's alive and well today at age thirty-three. How is this possible?
> **He was born in room 1955.**
>
> A word I know, six letters it contains, subtract just one, and twelve is what remains.
> **Dozens.**
>
> It walks on four legs in the morning, two legs at noon, and three legs in the evening. What is it?
> **Man.**
>
> Two in a corner, 1 in a room, 0 in a house, but 1 in a shelter. What am I?
> **The letter R.**
>
> One would cost a quarter. Twelve would cost fifty cents. One hundred twenty-two would cost seventy-five cents. When I left the store, I had spent seventy-five cents. What did I buy?
> **House numbers.**
>
> Two in a whole and four in a pair. And six in a trio, you see. And eight's a quartet but what you must get is the name that fits just one of me?
> **Half.**

Every single one of them had numbers in them. I wrote all the numbers out in order.

19 55 33 6 1 12 4 2 3 2 1 0 1 1 25 12 50 122 75 75 2 4 6 3 8 4 1

I typed the numbers into the website. And BOOM, I was in. It took me to an account landing page. I couldn't believe it. The jack-hole had been grooming me to find this money since I was eight. Unfortunately, all it showed was the account number, and right in the middle of the page, it asked me for a password.

I tried everything from "Delilah" to "happy" and everything in between. I typed in everything I could think of for hours.

I was near my wits' end. I rummaged through all of his files, ransacked all his papers, typed in every number and combination of letters I could think of.

Then I stumbled upon the cipher key.

His notebook. The one I found all those months ago. I made it all the way to Dad's list. The one thing that stood out in a book full of numbers.

For the first time, I noticed that some of the letters were all funky. 'm going to transcode it perfectly as it is on the page this time.

       Some Pretty Kickbutt AWeSome plANs BefORe i Die
       1. fly A kite with my DaughteR.
       2. Send a messAge 1n a bOttle.
       3. Eat mY wEight in chili.
       4. sOar without a pLane.
       5. haVe a tea paRty.
       6. catch the biggeSt fis4 1n the lake.
       7. Make the worLd's best sundae.
       8. win a cLassic car race.
       9. destroY soMething beautiful.

I unscrambled the letters in the bold heading to come up with **BANK PASSWORD.**

My dad's a crafty little devil, but it was simple once I figured out the code and unscrambled the letters.

When I finished, my eyes welled up with tears.

I'm going to put the answer WAY down on this page in case somebody wants to figure it out themselves.

WAY, WAY DOWN.

SERIOUSLY.

I don't want to give it away.

Keep going.

Alright. That's far enough. Here's what I got.

1AMS0RRYDEL1LA4MYLOVE

I don't know how he did it. I don't know why he did it. And that certainly didn't make it all better, but I'd be lying if I didn't say getting a message from beyond the grave wasn't touching in the slightest.

I typed in the password. The account opened up. I looked at the balance:

$1,000,000.

"Whoa," was all I could muster.

That is enough money to make us square with the house people, the tax people, the school people, and still have enough to buy and sell this town a couple times over.

It was a dream, a dream that was quickly shattered when I realized clueless Terrence had the same information I did.

He was probably sitting on the account waiting for somebody to open it.

Why did I give him all my evidence?!

Why had I been so thorough?!

THE BOX

Posted by Delilah Clark × May 22 at 9:53 pm.

I poked my head into Terrence's new, gigantic office for what I hoped would be the last time. After the huge bust, I basically handed to him, the top brass had no choice but to promote him, which was good for me, since I needed a favor.

Terrence groaned just like old times. "Shouldn't you be studying? You couldn't possibly need anything from me."

But I did. I needed to know about the money and what they were doing to track it down.

Terrence told me that since everybody related to the embezzlement was dead, neither the police nor the FBI cared about the money.

GroupThink doesn't care because they had all of their money insured to the hilt. They're making out better than if they'd just kept it in a bank. The only person who could care is the IRS, but they don't make a habit of going after dead guys.

I was confident that nobody would be the wiser about my dad's account if I kept the money, but it didn't make me feel any better about it.

Then I heard Terrence clear his throat. "I hear, though, that GroupThink is offering a 33 percent reward, no questions asked, for any information leading to the return of their money."

It was all very interesting. I really didn't know what to make of it. Should I keep the money, or should I return it?

That question is going to keep me up all night, maybe all week, until I figure out the right answer.

GIRL TALK

Posted by Alex Dewitt × May 23 at 5:15 pm.

Delilah was in a super-chipper mood today. Maybe it's because she's planned a date with Moses.

Like the Moses whom she hated. Seriously, I'm not screwing with you here. Apparently, Delilah's life-changing experiences have opened her up to more experiences.

Maybe it's because she figured out how she'll pay for Harvard, but she's not telling me how.

She said it's her secret. I probed and prodded, but at the end of the day she just said, "It's for your own good." and that was that.

It doesn't matter, really. I just like that she's hanging out with me again. She dyed her hair back to the blonde I loved, burned her black clothes, and bought a slew of new, pink, preppy clothes with some sort of money I didn't know about.

People haven't forgiven me for taking her side.

They haven't forgiven me for letting Moses have the credit for pulling off the dance and making him the savior either.

That's okay. At least I have Delilah and my pride. Even if she's all I have. Even if I have one friend. Then I'll be okay.

I used to need all the people, all the things, all the friends. But being without them showed me that I can do it alone. I can be alone. And I can survive.

Besides, when I win the state gymnastics meet next year, people will come around. They'll come begging.

DAD'S LETTER

Posted by Delilah Clark × May 24 at 9:14 pm.

I sat in front of the mirror, wet hair wrapped in a towel, primping for my date with Moses.

I still can't believe I'm dating him. I still can't believe I'm happy dating him.

I barely recognized myself. I'd returned my hair to its natural blonde.

I don't know which I like more. I'd grown accustomed to black hair, but at the end of the day, that wasn't me. I'm not sure about this blonde me either, though. Maybe I'll try blue next.

"It looks good," Mom said. Turning around, I saw her holding a note. "Your father left this for you. I found it clutched in his hand. I didn't think it was appropriate to let you read it. But after all you went through, I realized I was wrong."

I sat down on the bed and opened the letter. My heart dropped with every passing word.

> *Dearest Delilah,*
>
> *I know you won't understand what I must do, but please know that I love you deeply and with all my heart. I know you will grow up to be a woman of great courage, conviction, and strength. I only wanted the best for you. I may have gone about it the wrong way, but I wanted to give you everything. I love you very much. Goodbye.*
>
> *Dad*

I couldn't believe my eyes. I sat, mouth agape, for what must've been hours.

"I told you before that I knew for a fact he'd committed suicide. That note is why."

There was a long silence as she let it all sink in.

"It will be okay," Mom finally said. "We'll get through it."

I wiped the tears from my eyes. "Hey, I'm supposed to be saying that to you."

She shook her head. "No, baby. I'm finally doing it right."

BONFIRE

Posted by Delilah Clark × May 26 at 9:14 am.

I didn't tell Moses what we were doing in the woods. He probably thought I was gonna jump his bones.

Those are crazy thoughts though. After a couple dates and light petting, I don't think so, buddy.

We walked into the clearing where my dad's car still sat in a husk. I lifted a gallon of gasoline from the trunk and doused the car with it.

Moses stayed silent. I liked that about him. He didn't ask questions.

Then I lit a match and threw it inside the car. It wasn't long before the flames reached the heavens and ignited the night sky.

I leaned against Moses for a moment, enjoying the sound of his heart beating. When ready, I reached into my back pocket and pulled out my father's notebook. I chucked it into the fire.

No ceremony. No nothing. I just wanted it out of my life.

As its pages curled in the fire, I took out dad's note and looked it over one last time. Then, I crumpled it up and tossed it into the fire, too. As we watched it burn, I grabbed onto Moses's arm and pulled him close.

I was suddenly ravenous. I knew exactly what I could go for: a shared banana split and basket of fries.

And I knew just the place.

WORK

Posted by Delilah Clark × June 4 at 5:34 pm.

Sooooo... I'm in a bit of a pickle.

I want to go to Harvard, but I haven't been to school all year. Which means my grades are complete garbage.

Even with my first semester straight A's, I have to make up nearly a year of work before Harvard's going to let me grace them with my presence.

It's going to take all my focus. All my energy. And a lot of luck.

I'm going to have to call in every favor. Do everything in my power. And even then, I might be screwed.

So, you won't be hearing from me much. That better not affect my grade.

SUMMATION

Posted by Delilah Clark × June 9 at 5:13 pm.

This was quite a year. Quite a year indeed.

There are lots of things I feel bad about, but I feel the worst about Alex—I completely abandoned her for months.

I've spent a lot of time in these last weeks trying to rebuild that trust, but I think it might be broken forever.

I just hope one day she'll forgive me.

It's in that vein I want to end this accursed year; talking about forgiveness. Forgiveness for my father. There's a saying I heard a long time ago:

"Forgive others, not because they deserve forgiveness, but because you deserve peace."

I'll never get to the point of forgetting my dad's transgressions. I never will, nor would I want to.

What he did was horrible. What he did destroyed me, my family, my friendships, and my life. He claimed to do it all out of love, but how can somebody cause so much misery to those he claimed to love?

No. I'll never forget it, but I can forgive it. Not because he deserves forgiveness, but because I deserve it.

And I can forgive myself for holding my dad up on a pedestal. He wasn't a demon, nor was he a saint. He wasn't a great man, or even a good one. He was just a flawed man. A very flawed, pained, hurt man. I'm sure he had dreams beyond GroupThink, maybe even beyond me. He talked of travel, of independence, and of love. He always had love. He wanted me to have love, too. He wanted me to love him.

And I will always love him. And I can forgive him. If not for him, then at least for my own peace.

My pendulum swings from one extreme to the other and will someday settle in the middle. I had such reverence for Dad.

When that glass shattered, it shattered hard.

But I'll learn.

Nobody is as evil or as good as you see them—not Bennett, not Terrence, not Mom, not even Alex. Although Alex is closest. She's the bomb, Donkey Kong.

SAYING GOOD-BYE

Posted by Alex Dewitt × August 3 at 11:02 pm.

Delilah is finally gone to Harvard.

Not only did it take her two straight months to make up all the work she missed, but Mr. Willis and about a dozen teachers had to call Harvard on her behalf. He gave them an ear full about her situation, and she got there for the last two weeks of the program.

I miss her already. I know she'll be back in a few weeks. But the craziness had just finally died down for us.

There was time for us to just be...us. I had my friend back. Now I've lost her again. I know it's only for a short time, but—

I don't know. I feel alone again, and I was just starting to not feel like that.

She told me she'd write, but we both know Harvard is Harvard. It's a new world with new experiences. At least I'll have her back for the school year.

I'll still hang out with Kendra. She invites me over every night for dinner. I'm sure I'll take her up on it more often than not. She's bouncing back faster these days. She's got a job as a DMV clerk. She's even talking about getting into a trade school to become a medical assistant.

Mom is headed home to pick me up for a trip to Thailand, and gymnastics starts when I get back. There are plenty of new things to keep me occupied. Mom always comes at the least opportune times, never when I need her. I doubt I'll even tell her about this year, how hard it was, or that I needed her. That's just the way it is.

And with that, I bid you farewell. I got my A. It was the only A I got this year, so thanks for that. I hope I didn't piss you off too much with what I wrote.

AT HARVARD

Posted by Delilah Clark × August 10th at 11:14 pm.

It's been a while, huh. Things at the end of the year were hectic.

I basically spent every waking moment studying or taking exams. I had to take both sessions of summer school, beg, plead, grovel, and cry, but the school superintendent finally relented and let me make up all the work I missed.

I don't think I slept for two straight months.

It was a breakneck pace, but I got it done! I'm actually typing this from Harvard, in my very own dorm room, with my very own slightly weird roommate, who I don't like very much. But that's okay, because she doesn't like me much, either.

The funny thing is—she's a Goth!

I mean that's not really that funny, but it is pretty amusing. She thinks that I'm this preppy nerd who has never dyed my hair, or tried to kill herself, or seen a dead body. How ironic is that?! When I tell her what I did the past year, she's going to flip! We might go from mortal enemies to besties.

I have so much to tell you.

First and foremost, Harvard is everything I expected it to be and more. The people are so smart and cool and nice.

They talk about Proust like my friends at home talk about Probst.

My classes are so hard, they've got my brain spinning and hurting, but only in the best way. Every class is filled with either trust fund jerks or super overachievers like myself.

Guess which group I've been drawn to so far?

Second, I got an A on my online diary.

It was so successful my teacher told me he's going to force everybody to do it online next year.

YAY!

I pulled him into the new millennium. Of course, I don't expect anybody else's to be as good or interesting as mine, but one can only hope. Or not hope, I guess. Wouldn't want anybody to go through what I went through.

Alex is rockin' and rollin' with her gymnastics. She's got a newfound confidence and is competing in nationals this year!

Olympics 2016 here she comes!!!

Moses and I are still together, kind of. Well, we're together in the way that any new couple could be together from a thousand miles away. He sends me candy and worries I'm going to leave him for some college jack-hole. That's not going to happen, of course, no matter how jacked the hole is. We'll see how it goes when I go back home after summer school.

Mom actually got a job. She's working as a clerk at the DMV. I don't really know what she does, but it gets her out of the house. We talk every day.

We're no longer behind on the mortgage, and with my dad's vicious spending binges no longer an issue, I think she might actually have more money coming in now than before. She's talking about enrolling in a trade school, so she can better herself. I'm so proud of her.

I know everybody's wondering what I did with the money. Did I keep it or give it back? I have to tell you it was a hard decision at first, but then I realized something.

Terrence is notoriously an idiot. There's no way that the FBI, police, and about ninety different agencies wouldn't be looking for a million dollars.

And besides, I'm not a thief. I may be half my father, but I left that out of the equation, thank you very much.

I wasn't about to jeopardize my future for some money. Besides, the consolation prize of $333K tax-free allowed us to pay off all the debt my dad accumulated and dig deep into our mortgage. Mom won't have to worry about that for a while. I was even able to keep enough to somewhat pay for the college experience.

Don't get me wrong, I'll have to work six jobs to even pay my room and board when I come here full time, but it was worth it to not have the cops on my back watching my every move.

I don't think I'll ever be that chipper, bouncy person I was before my dad died, but I won't be that miserable person from the last year either. I'll be somewhere in the middle, and eventually the pain of his death and betrayal will dissipate...I hope.

With that, I come to some sad news. This will be the last post I'm going to put up for a while, maybe ever.

This blog was so cathartic and wonderful. It kept me going during the worst of times and allowed me to say things I could never say in person. It allowed me to document the worst year, hopefully, of my entire life, and I'll always treasure it for that.

But life is for the living. And memories are for the making. It's time for me to quit living on my computer and get out there. I turned to writing when things were at their worst, and now that life has improved, I am going to step off the gas and go back to enjoying things. Toodles!

*

If you liked that, then make sure to check out *Sorry for Existing,* also set in East Willow, except in a much different part of the town.

Sorry for Existing is about a disabled boy who meets a homeless alien and helps her rebuild her ship so she can get off the planet.

*

Now, here's a preview of Sorry for Existing.

ONE

It started with a bang and a whimper.

Well it wasn't really a bang.

It was more like a slap. Well, exactly like a slap.

Actually, it wasn't really a slap either. It was – what's the sound a fist makes when it connects with a woman's jaw? Like a woomp, or a thud, or a thwonk.

Well, that was the sound. The sound of my mother being punched across the jaw by my father; her hair, her body, suspended motionless for a second, then falling gracefully in slow motion, as I watched horrified and petrified, nestled in the corner behind her.

He'd aimed for me, but Mom jumped between us so that I wouldn't face his assault. She always did that.

She told me that the initial blow was always the worst; that she became numb after the third or fourth hit.

At least that's what she told me. I never believed her. I too often saw the pain on her face when he kicked her ribs for the eighth and ninth times. I watched helpless as the tears welled in her eyes. It was hell.

Dad screamed the vilest things imaginable while he beat her. I blocked out the worst of it through years of willful self-delusion. But a few burrowed deep into my memory. I used to wake at night, drenched in cold sweat. His screams jolted me out of my daydreams. They snapped me back to reality.

"You vile, worthless WHORE!"

"Lying sack of shit!"

"Dumb Bitch!"

Those were his favorites. She would cry and cry, for hours it seemed, until giant snot bubbles came out of her nose. He punched, kicked, screamed, and stomped my mother within inches of her life on more than a dozen occasions.

She spent weeks in the hospital, battling to breathe, hoping to die. Punctured lungs, broken noses, and cracked rib cages became the norm; police reports and flimsy denials, standard operating procedure. He didn't like lies, but truths only made him madder and the beatings more vicious. After a spell we kept our mouth shut and did our bid –hoping to one day get paroled.

*

Mom wouldn't let him take out his anger on me. Not on her twelve-year old baby with an oxygen tank; not to the little kid whose simple existence was a miracle. Not to the kid that she made this way.

And I don't mean in the way her egg and his sperm did the freaky-deeky so I could eventually be popped out nine months later.

Though of course that's 100% accurate in the most literal sense. I mean you could interpret it that way for sure. But more so my condition was brought on by their negligence.

I have a condition called pulmonary fibrosis. There's a couple of causes from genetics to environmental factors. It basically meant my lungs were all messed up, scarred over, and didn't work right. If they worked worse, I'd be on a lung transplant list, but they work just well enough that I'll just have shitty lung disease for the rest of my shortened life.

Now, one of the causes of pulmonary fibrosis could have been my mother smoking during pregnancy. As much as I'd love to blame her for that, she took impeccable care while I baked inside her. She didn't smoke, took prenatal vitamins, listened to classical music, and stayed away from fish. She didn't even drink. Not one drop. It wasn't until after my diagnosis that the pills and booze took hold.

No, the cause of my condition comes from being poor; really, really poor; so poor that we couldn't afford adequate housing. Poor enough to squat anyplace that accepted our meager cash, even if it meant buildings riddled with asbestos.

As a child I was susceptible to all sorts of things that my parents' immune system could withstand.

I'm 18 now.

I was 12 during this story.

I was 8 when they diagnosed me.

That's the worst part. My condition wasn't some genetic defect. It wasn't some moment-of-birth botch. It wasn't something I'd lived with my entire life.

I remember being a normal kid; playing sports, running, jumping, living outside a protective cocoon. I remember biting into a fresh apple without tasting sand. I remember breathing without pins and needles stabbing my lungs. I remember a life where my parents didn't blame themselves for my existence, where even for a moment we were blissfully happy.

I mean blissfully happy. Over the moon, laugh every night, Norman Rockwell, Kodak stock portrait happy. The kind of happy we would nauseatingly shake our heads at today. The kind of happy that breaks my heart to think about, because I can never have it again.

Seven though, that was a magical year. Dad came home every night to a warm cooked meal. He regaled Mom with stories of his day as she sat enthralled on the edge of her seat. We made pillow forts and watched old movies that went way over my head, all cuddled up around the shitty CRT Dad found at a yard sale. We were dirt poor. We didn't care though. We didn't need things to be happy. We just needed to be together.

It wasn't meant to last though. I started getting winded at soccer practice, then I could barely make it home from school. My chest began to burn and ache throughout the day and into the night. Then, the wretched coughing started, followed by the blood.

We went to doctor after doctor after doctor and our meager finances ran dry, but Mom and Dad were vigilant. They endured any cost, no matter how high, to ensure that my health was sound.

Specialist after specialist shook their head and confirmed my parents' worst fears. By my eighth birthday it was a foregone conclusion. They didn't get me toys, or video games, or even books. They got me two shiny oxygen tanks. I still use them to this day. Happy Birthday to me, right?

*

As you can imagine, having a kid that lived off oxygen tanks, with hardly any immune system, all because you couldn't afford a nicer place, puts a strain on a marriage financially, emotionally, and physically; even to the most well-adjusted, intelligent, and/or thoughtful among us.

My father was none of the above. Seeing a constant reminder of his shortcomings was too much for him to handle. He, who was supposed to protect me, instead created a feeble monster – kept alive by tubes and machines.

It pissed him off. It pissed him off more every time he looked at me. He was too simple, too stupid, and too cowardly to look inside himself – to beat himself, so he redirected it out onto everybody around him. He was once a gentle giant, now he was consumed by rage.

My mother's love, on the other hand, collapsed upon itself like a neutron star. She grew numb and callused. She gave freely and unrepentantly to my father, who for decades fed off that love to make it through the day. When his rage boiled over, she loved harder and harder. Surely her love could bring him back from the brink. Surely, they could get through this together. Surely, she would not have to go it alone.

No matter how much she gave, it fell into a black hole of rage and bitterness. He shunned her, ignored her, berated her, and eventually beat her when she tried to reason with him. It's very hard to love a man that changed so violently and so quickly. She gave everything of herself away to him and she had nothing left for the child that needed it.

All she could do was use her numb, powerless body to take a beating for me. She had no other way to show her love. She'd given it all away, and my disease overloaded her circuits. It overloaded both of their circuits. I was the surge that fried their marriage.

What a shitty place for an eight-year old to be.

*

Mom was a night owl by necessity if not by choice. She hated sleep. More so, she hated dreaming. Once she dreamed of nice homes, butterflies, and fairy tales; that her life would be better, hopeful, possibly, even kind.

Those dreams soured in my ninth year and curdled in my twelfth. By then she hated dreams, not for the nightmares, which showed her the true horrors of her mind, but for the dreams, which filled her with the hope of a better life. There was no better life for Mom, and she hated the flutter in her stomach that accompanied that moment of wakening where she believed her dreams were realities.

Cheap wine helped. Lots of cheap wine. She wasn't picky. It never filled her with restful sleep, but it blocked her dreams from invading her reality. Five, six, some nights eight glasses of wine would be the only thing that allowed her to sleep. When we couldn't afford wine, she skimmed my pills. She skimmed a lot of pills. I learned to live in pain to numb hers.

*

The night after her vicious beating she wandered up to bed early, nursing her wounds. I begged her to call an ambulance, but she refused.

"I know my own body, Sammy. I'm fine," she assured me. One day those words will be emblazoned on her tombstone. "You can get to bed yourself tonight."

Mom never let me get myself to bed. Something was amiss. Every night she tucked me in, kissed me on the cheek, and pulled the oxygen mask over my face.

Oxygen masks are uncomfortable to sleep in. The plastic tube tickled my fingers or wrapped around my turning body, waking me abruptly and unkindly.

I stopped wearing them most nights. Lying in bed never did much to aggravate my condition. My heart calmed, my breathing slowed, and my body stopped shaking profusely. Only my mind raced faster in the darkness.

*

I never slept well. I tossed and turned. I twitched and fidgeted. I sighed and harrumphed. I jerked awake and laid silently for hours. I peeked into hallways and listened for fights, whether arguments or bare-knuckle brawls. I stared at the ceiling or out the window toward the stars, wishing I could get lost in them forever. I waited patiently for an ambulance or a weekly run to the emergency room.

In those rare instances when I slept early and deeply – when the stars aligned, and the sleep fairies released me from their dance between awake and sleep – those were undoubtedly the nights when I woke gasping for air.

Those nights worried me the most – ironically, they kept me up more than any other. I hated choking and gasping for every molecule of air. But more than that, I feared an oxygen tank exploding in the night and killing me in my sleep – or worse, leaving me disfigured and even more crippled. I feared I would never wake up and I feared I would.

*

I enjoyed dreams though, when they came. My imagination was the only place I could become normal again. My dreams weren't filled with the knights, Dark Knights, spaceships, fantasies, or wild pursuits that accompanied most peoples' dreams. They were filled with the simple moments, the lost moments, the hopeful moments that were never meant to be.

I dreamed of my fourth birthday, when my Father built a swing set out of discarded lumber. The stupid thing wouldn't sit straight, and after a week it crumbled to the ground. "But I built it, Sammy. You have to give me credit for that."

I did, of course. It did little to offset the brutality of his later years, but he did get credit for being a good father eight years of my life. I dreamt often of him carrying me around the house in his arms when I was just a tiny poop machine. He sang to me; terribly, of course, but he sang to me. The look of love in his eyes in those dreams, I tried to hold onto that, remember that there used to be a warm-hearted man where now a cold, brutal monster lurked.

Dreams never filled me with the pain and suffering they elicited in my mom. Dreams were what my life should have been, could have been, might have been, and one day might be again. I know it was a stupid thing to hope, but hope is all somebody sickly has most days, most moments of most days. Pills, injections, doctors, abuses, and constant pain drove you insane, something had to pull you back from the edge. For me, it was those dreams.

*

It was well past midnight when her frail hands jostled me awake. I'd been deep in a dream about my father teaching me how to grip a baseball bat. Mom clamped my lips tight. "Get up. And be quiet about it."

"But—"

"Don't question me! Just do it!" I hadn't heard my mother stern in a long time.

Her frail desperation masked the fire of a warrior; a determined, stoic yeoman. Most people, places, things, and even ideas would have petered and died when faced with the hell she dealt with on a daily basis.

"Stay quiet," she said. "Grab your oxygen tanks."

"Where are we—?"

"Just grab them, alright?"

I scooped up my two tanks into their ripped backpack case and squeezed her hand. Her pulse thumped loudly through her cadaverous fingers.

"Careful," she whispered over her shoulders. "Only step where I step."

I mimicked her pointed feet as we tiptoed down the hallway and down the stairs toward the front lawn. It was slow going. My mother calculated every move carefully, tiptoeing over the cracks and loose floorboards of the landlord's shoddy, ramshackle house.

Every move she made was masterful, a stroke of genius. It was as if a ballerina replaced my mother. She knew which floorboard wouldn't creak and where the safest landings were. She slid ever so carefully down the banister so that the middle three stairs wouldn't squeak – and jumped off centimeters before it swayed and cracked.

We eventually reached the front door. She swung it open just enough to avoid tipping off the rusty hinges and slid me outside. Her face peeked out of the door, then disappeared back inside.

"Run!" she screamed through the partially closed door. I stood frozen for seconds that felt like years. I heard Mom's ragdoll body crash against the door with a heavy thump.

My feet separated from my brain and rushed forward on their own. They slammed into the door once, twice, three times. My brain knew it was a bad idea, but the rest of my body didn't care. My tiny, frail body reared back a fourth time and finally crashed through the door.

The force knocked Dad over. He stumbled backward against the staircase.

"You little shit!" he screamed.

Mom stuffed her keys in my hand and shoved me back out the door. "Go! Start the car!"

I'd never done anything like that before, but I obeyed. My chest burned with a fire I hadn't felt in a long time; panic, excitement, my lungs collapsing. I had to fight through it. My mom's life depended on it. I saw the fire in my dad's eyes. Rage overtook him completely. There was no semblance of humanity in him, nothing could hold back his fury. If I didn't get Mom out tonight, she'd be dead by morning.

I heard her scream again and again as I fumbled with the keys. I managed to open the door and slide into the driver's seat. Mom's belabored breath struggling out a whimper through the door. "Hurry."

The neighborhood's normally darkened porches suddenly illuminated. I didn't care. My father didn't care. Even the neighbors didn't care. They just wanted to make sure that their cars weren't being robbed or vandalized.

I stuck the key in the ignition and turned until the car puttered to life. Mom sprinted out the front door. "It's on," I shouted. "Hurry up!!!"

"Move over!" she yelled.

I scooted myself into the passenger seat just as she jumped inside; her nose bled; her eye swelled. She wheezed in pain as she threw the car into reverse and tore out of the driveway, taking the mailbox with her and barely missing a neighbor's cat.

My father leapt out of the front door and flung himself on the car as my mother shifted the car into drive.

"Whore! You dumb, freaking whore," he screamed. "Stop this car right now or I'm gonna kill you!!!"

Mom clenched her eyes closed and floored the gas pedal. Dad lost his balance and crashed into the windshield. He bounced as we sped up and hit the roof, caving it under his massive weight.

He rolled off the trunk, limp and motionless. The last thing I remember was watching my father lay on the ground, blood pooling around him.

I hoped he was dead.

*

If you liked that preview, make sure to pick up *Sorry for Existing* today!

ALSO BY RUSSELL NOHELTY

THE SHITIVERSE

The Gods' Sin

The Immortal's Doom

The Pixie's Promise

The Devil's Circle

OTHER WORK

My Father Didn't Kill Himself

Sorry for Existing

The Little Bird and the Little Worm

Gumshoes: The Case of Madison's Father

The Invasion Saga

The Marked Ones

The Vessel

Worst Thing in the Universe

The Void Calls Us Home

GRAPHIC NOVELS AND COMIC BOOKS

Ichabod Jones: Monster Hunter

Katrina Hates the Dead

Gherkin Boy

Pixie Dust